THE 6:41 TO PARIS

JEAN-PHILIPPE BLONDEL

Translated by
ALISON ANDERSON

NEW VESSEL PRESS
NEW YORK

THE 6:41 TO PARIS

New Vessel Press

www.newvesselpress.com

First published in French in 2013 as *06h41*
Copyright © 2013 Libella, Paris
Translation Copyright © 2015 Alison Anderson

Library of Congress Cataloging-in-Publication Data
Blondel, Jean-Philippe
[06h41. English]
The 6:41 to Paris/Jean-Philippe Blondel; translation by Alison Anderson.
p. cm.
ISBN 978-1-939931-26-9
Library of Congress Control Number 2015935267
     I. France -- Fiction

The 6:41 to Paris

I could have taken the 7:50, or even the 8:53. It's Monday. Mondays are dead quiet at work. It's just that I couldn't take it anymore. What was I thinking, staying Sunday night. I don't know what came over me. Two days are more than enough.

I didn't sleep well at all last night, obviously. I was so annoyed with myself. Another wasted weekend. And at the same time, it was no surprise, it's always like that. Valentine could have told me it would be. So could Luc. And I understand their perspective, but it pisses me off. That they didn't come. That they didn't do their bit. That they weren't there supporting me so I could get through those two days. That they don't care as much about my parents as I do. Which is normal. They are *my* parents. My very own. My only parents, and I'm their only daughter.

Every time, I swear it can't go on like this. And then I start feeling guilty. Insidiously. I hear their voices on the phone. Never a reproach. Never a complaint. Just silence, when I say that I have a lot of work at the moment. I have to get in touch with my suppliers. I have to satisfy my clients. I can just imagine them on the other end of the line. My mother standing ramrod straight behind my father. Brittle. The grimace on her face. The scathing remark on the tip of her tongue. I wonder if there is anyone anywhere who knows how to look after elderly parents. Elderly but not yet bedridden.

Just old and weak. Old and vulnerable. And bitter.

No, actually, I don't wonder. There must be somebody, yes. Luc, for example. Except actually he doesn't care about them at all. He severed all connections with his family more than twenty years ago, and apart from a very occasional visit or phone call, he's not in touch. I think that's what I admired most about him when we met. How independent he could be. That salutary selfishness. I admired it even more than his presence. Or his style. The style he has kept in spite of the passage of time. He's pushing fifty, but he's still slim, trim, almost rugged. The kind of man that women over forty dream about. I'm not jealous. I never have been. I'm not submissive enough. Our mutual independence is both a challenge and a source of respect.

Naturally my parents complained when Luc didn't show up. It's not that he's overly friendly with them, but they like it better when we come *as a family*. With Luc and Valentine. That way they can tell the entire neighborhood—the shopkeepers in particular—"Last weekend, the whole family was here." They like saying that, *the whole family*.

This time, the other two members of *the whole family* didn't give in.

I tried to explain. Luc had a lot of work, his company is in the middle of a restructuring. And as for Valentine, you know … As a rule, just saying "you know …" and following it with a sigh should be enough, should suggest the fact that Valentine is almost seventeen, she lives just outside Paris, she's in love, and she hates coming to this town out in the boonies where she doesn't know a soul and where her grandpa is constantly sending her out into the garden to play as if she were still seven years old.

But that's not enough for my parents. I have to come up with a pretty lie, neatly packaged, festooned with magnificent lemon yellow ribbons—and served up with a radiant smile. I'm used to it. I learned to hide the truth from them very early on. So I invented some fake exams for Valentine on Monday morning, that way all day Sunday she'd have to be studying for them. When I told her how I planned to lie to her grandparents, she burst out laughing, hugged me, and asked why I didn't just tell them that whenever she went there she got so bored she could die and that they were a real pain in the butt. I didn't say anything. The only thing I could think of was "I couldn't speak like that to my parents," but I didn't come out with it because I know for a fact that Luc and Valentine would be perfectly capable of saying something like that.

I wonder if Valentine will talk to us like that later on. When it's our turn to wait for her visit in our little house in the suburbs. No, no suburbs. I'm not going to get old in the Paris suburbs. I don't come from there. There's nothing to keep me there. I've started thinking about where I—I mean *we*, if all goes well—might end our days. I like the thought of Mexico, or Morocco, but I know I would miss books and movies and my own language. And besides, I know those countries. I've already been there. I'm glad I was able to visit them, but

I can't see myself living there. No. I need a quiet place. Flat, open country—but with hills on the horizon, all the same. Or else the sea. The ocean, rather. Salty, wild, sticking to your skin. But not Paris. No. Or here, either. Troyes. The Champagne region. I've had enough of it. On the station platform. 6:35. I can't begin to think how many times I've waited for a train under this glass roof.

It's stupid.

Everything is stupid.

The fact I got up so early. And stayed an extra night, above all. I had the choice. I could have gone home last night—but I don't know, the thought of forty-five minutes on the Métro and RER and then getting home from the Gare de l'Est, and then all over again in the other direction on Monday morning really depressed me. And my mother's face, transformed into this Mater Dolorosa, stubbornly silent of course, at the thought of my departure on Sunday afternoon. I knew that Valentine was sleeping over at Éléonore's and that Luc would be spending the evening on his computer. So I clapped my hands, like a little girl, and blurted, "I'll just leave on Monday morning!" I called Luc, who grumbled. And sent a text to Valentine—in any case, there's no other way to get in touch with her. Her reply: "OK. Hugs." There comes an age when you find yourself trapped between indifferent children and recalcitrant parents. That's all there is to it. I'm forty-seven years old. I'm right in the middle of it.

In the end, my parents were more surprised than anyone. Unpleasantly surprised. Especially my mother.

The Mater Dolorosa became a Mater Anxiosa. This would upset her routine. This would give her multiple causes for concern. She wouldn't be able to put the sheets I had used into the washing machine. It would throw everything off. And what on earth will we have for supper, we didn't plan, did we, Sunday evening, you know, usually it's just soup, the police show on Channel 2, and off to bed! And besides, what's behind it? Is there something wrong between you and Luc? That's why he didn't come, isn't it! Oh, you know you can come out and tell us, but you could be a little nicer to him, after all. It's as if you always decide everything.

So I had to fight back. I said, "Aren't you pleased I'm spending some time with you?" They beat a hasty retreat. They apologized. They said, Of course, it's just that … No point in taking it any further. I know. *The whole family*. And to think that, in my everyday life, I am respected. Almost feared. I plan. I decide. I hire.

I don't know if I'll be sad when they pass away.

Apparently you can boast about your indifference, but when that time comes, the emotion just comes straight at you and mows you down. Whatever. I find it hard to believe. In short, a completely wasted weekend. All I did was go around in circles in my parents' house. The only time I got out was to go and change my train ticket yesterday—oh, and I also went with my mother to the boulangerie-pâtisserie which isn't a boulangerie and even less of a patisserie, but just a place where they sell bread. She wanted to buy some custard. For dessert on

Sunday evening. Since nothing had been planned.

It goes without saying that I won't share any of this with Luc. It would only prove that he was right and he would go around with his smug little smile on his face. Nor will I say a word to Valentine—she doesn't care, anyway. Nor do my colleagues. And the few friends we still have—it's crazy how once people turn forty friendships seem to disintegrate. They get transferred, they're busy with their kids, you no longer share the same opinions—everything alienates you from people you thought would be close to you all your life. All that's left are laconic email messages. Phone calls punctuated with long silences. Sporadic meetings.

No. Stop.

I have to remind myself that when I haven't slept well I get all bent out of shape. It's 6:41 in the morning, after all. And I'm in a foul mood.

I'm astonished how many people are here. And how many trains there are this early. It's as if half the town were going to work in Paris every day.

Which may well be the case.

Here comes the train—on time. Thank goodness.

I would have gone crazy if it had been late.

I like trains. All the time you can spend doing nothing in particular. You get your bag ready for the trip—like with kids when they're still small. You pack two paperbacks, some chewing gum, a bottle of water—you can almost imagine putting your security blanket in there, too. Everything you need to pass the time pleasantly. When you get to the station, you even linger at the newsstand, you buy a magazine, preferably one about the rich and famous. It's as if you were going to the beach—and like at the beach, you end up not bothering with the novels or the magazine, you don't chew on the gum and you even forget to drink the water. You get hypnotized by the landscape rolling by, or the rhythm of the waves.

The only train I can't stand is on Sunday night to Paris. When I was a student, that train meant depression and uprooting. I would get to the Gare de l'Est feeling totally dispirited. Because my roots are here. I've always known that. I was like the rooster in the farmyard back here. In Paris I was nobody. But it was all so long ago. That doesn't stop me hating the Sunday night train. That's why I'm here so early this morning. I could have taken the 9:25 last night and slept at Mathieu's place, since I have the keys. But I didn't feel like it. I would rather set the alarm and get up and head for the train station when it's still dark. There are dozens of shadows like me on the way. Except that they do it every day. For me it's an exception. The later trains get into Paris too late—at 10:30, 11:30, the morning is already half over and you feel as if you're showing up in the middle of the party.

A day unlike any other.
Unique.
A break with routine.
I start at the store at 10:00 on Mondays and I'm at it until seven in the evening. In a while I'll phone from Paris to say I can't come in today. I'll make up the hours; there's a family emergency. I know the secretary on the other end of the line will be worried. In twenty years working at the superstore I haven't missed a single day—except when I had lumbago, four years ago. I'll promise to explain when I get back, tomorrow. Because I will get back tomorrow. In principle. Otherwise I'll have to find a doctor who'll give me a few days off. I wonder if Jérôme could do that. Maybe he could, after all. It would be strange. But Jérôme is so kind. More than that. He's a saint. A saint who took in my wife and kids after the divorce. And since then, he's been there to make sure they have a friendly environment, full of the comfort and warmth which were singularly lacking in their original family toward the end.

Except that, in fact, the divorce was because of him. No, that's unfair. It's much more complicated than that. Christine and I weren't getting along very well. We got on each other's nerves. She felt like she was wasting her life. She began to spend her evenings on the Internet, reconnecting with people. Finding friends from her teenage years. Her first love, whom she'd never completely forgotten. Jérôme, in other words. Who was divorced, too, no kids, a bit of a player but ready to settle down. They didn't even need Match.com. It's pathetic.

The kids were annoyed, but not actually all that much. The atmosphere in the house had been unbearable. Jérôme's dowry came with a much bigger house, and a sizable yard, where there was even some talk of putting in a swimming pool. He was kind and considerate, and he never said no to buying them magazines. He played video games. The perfect father. Manon was eight, Loïc was six. That was ten years ago. It all went very smoothly. For them. And for me? I don't think about it. I go on doing what I set out to do—except that I've kind of lost the purpose of the journey. I had a few promising but short-lived affairs. Of the kind that are good for your health. The months have gone by. The years. And I'm hardly likely to change the course of things now. I have my routine. The occasional phone call to Christine, as friendly as it is rare. The kids every other weekend until this year, when they asked for greater autonomy, and they don't spend their weekends with me or their mother, but with people we hardly know. As for half of the vacation this year, that could be a problem, too. Manon will be working at the outdoor sports center and her brother wants to take a sailing course for three weeks. I didn't fight it. That's not my style. I wait for my kids to feel guilty. That's my strategy. Needless to say, it's pretty useless. Next year, Manon is moving to Reims to study to become a physical therapist. That's what she wants to be. When I ask her why, she shrugs. She talks about money, clients, combining business with pleasure, doing good—and besides, it's a profession that should be safe from unemployment. She's reasonable. Can be a little cold. She's into sports. She's putting money aside so she won't have to be totally dependent on her parents and stepfather next year. Irreproachable. What ever happened to the little girl I used to fling into the public swimming pool singing *"Karma karma karma karma karma chameleon"* while she burst out laughing? But I'm being unfair. I doubt she's like that with her mother. Or with Jérôme. It's just something she has with her father. Loïc is headed down the same path. Only worse. He wants to be an orthodontist. What a magnificent dream for a sixteen-year-old.

Having said that, what were my dreams when I was sixteen? I didn't have any. I just let myself go with the flow. I was seizing the day, as they say. I was fed and housed and watered, I went out with girls, I spent time with my friends, and I thought life would always be like that.

I have to stop sighing.

I've noticed that I've been sighing more and more often. And that I get out of breath, and huff and puff. A bad sign. For a start, it drives others away, they get your number—a loser through and through. No one wants to talk to someone who sighs all the time, what if they start venting and go on for hours? And then you see yourself in a very unflattering light. Particularly as I'm only forty-seven. I just had my birthday. I have at least three more decades to get through. Without sighing.

Are these other people on the platform sighing?

It just goes to show, all these people at this time of day. The town never recovered from the loss of the textile industry or the joys of outsourcing. They've been trying to make the switch to the service sector—call centers, tourism, shipping—but the job market is tight and the jobs that are available are not very appealing. It's better to work in Paris all day long and deal with a three hour daily commute to earn a decent salary rather than put up with a schedule from hell to speak to some caller on a hotline.

At the end of his life my father worked in Paris. Promotion, career, money, prestige. He had it all figured out. He made his choice. He saw his wife and kids only two hours in the evening and two days on the weekend. It was just a question of months or a few years—and then they'd move south for their retirement, build a little house, it was all planned out, ordained, on course. But then one day he had a heart attack, when he was changing Métro lines. Defibrillators didn't exist back then. There were calls for help, people rushing over, gathering around, someone shouted, "I'm a doctor!" like in some second-rate TV show. But it wasn't enough. For three years my mother was inconsolable, and then she met this charming bicycle salesman who had just gotten divorced. They went on long rides together.

I'm aware that history is repeating itself.

I'm trying to fight it.

I figure that bicycle salesmen and doctors are not the same thing.

Or are they?

I also figure that I got divorced before, that I won't kill myself working, and that I won't end up dead in a Métro passageway. Unless I do today.

No.

I close my eyes while the ubiquitous female voice announces the arrival of the train in the station. I'd like to meet her someday, that woman. I wonder what she's like in real life. Does she spend her time recording messages such as "train number one thousand three hundred (pause) and fifty is currently delayed by (pause) five minutes?" How does she see her future? What does she like to do when she's not at work?

Above all I wonder how long this recorded voice has been making its announcements to passengers. I remember a day just like this. All those years ago. I took the same train—or its twin brother. I was seventeen. With Mathieu. It was the end of April, just like today. Easter vacation. We were leaving for Les Landes for a few days, to go camping. We'd been dreaming about our week on the coast for months. All the other students were green with envy. We were freedom personified. If I let myself go a little, I can even feel the weight of the tent and the backpack on my shoulders. And the impression I had that the whole world was opening up to me.

It was a disappointment. The campsite was deserted, so was the resort, there was nothing to do except go cycling in the dunes. The sea was still freezing and the beach hadn't been cleaned. You had to watch out for the clumps of tar that had collected in the sand. In the end we went home one day early, relieved to be among company and laughter and noise. Or at least I was. I don't know about Mathieu. He has always been very nostalgic about that vacation. He has often gone back to that stretch of coast. The only nostalgia I feel is for the moment of departure.

I could do it all over again today.

After all, no one is really expecting me. I disappear. My kids miss me a little, but mainly they are disturbed by the fact they don't know if I'm alive or dead. So I send them a postcard to reassure them. They go on with their lives. They notice that my absence doesn't make that much difference. At my work, they are concerned, then they react. Before long they brand me a deserter and I am fired. They find someone younger and more energetic to replace me, and who smiles more. In the meantime I'm up in the air and I land far away—in a place where the tumult of the world might still seem like just a faint whisper—Mongolia, Bolivia, a country like that, somewhere I've never been to. I had plans to travel. A lot of plans. And then, I don't know, one thing led to another, work, marriage, children, divorce. Most of the time purchasing power didn't go far enough. Neither did courage. I never made it very far. Spain twice, with the kids, to those concrete-covered resorts. Ireland, because Christine wanted to go there—I thought we'd find unspoiled nature and we'd be able to walk for miles without meeting another soul, and I found myself in the Mecca of European tourism. Florence, when I was young.

Until I was twenty-five, I crisscrossed France by train

because my dad worked for the national railway so I had a hefty discount on tickets. But there wasn't much of a discount once you crossed the border. And I didn't have anyone to go with me. So most of the time I stayed in France. There was that trip to Florence. Another to London. And a week in Brussels. Not much to show. I've never even set foot in the United States, despite the fact that I used to go on about how much I wanted to see America.

I could start traveling now.

I could transform the Métro into the regional RER. Paris into Charles de Gaulle airport. Mathieu into the rest of the world. My head is spinning, sort of. Not what I expected when I left the house this morning.

Shit.

It nearly made me forget to get on the train.

Here I am, dreaming of escape, and I almost got left behind on the platform.

The doors slammed shut right behind my back.

That was a close one.

I love to hear the sound of the doors closing. It signals the beginning of an egocentric and self-indulgent interlude. For the next two hours, nothing can really happen to you. Everything is taken care of. You can decide to immerse yourself in a novel, or succumb to the trance of the music coming from your headphones. You can also vanish into the screen of your laptop, into emails, spreadsheets, numbers, reports, and establish a direct yet disembodied connection with the outside world.

I don't do any of that. I daydream. Train journeys are rare opportunities to let go and lower my guard. Whereas in the Métro or the RER I can't do that. I'm always on the alert.

The seat next to me has not been taken.
It stays empty.
The train starts to move.
I'm of two minds.

On the one hand, I'm relieved. It's true that it's a bit weird, the closeness you get in a railroad car. You're only a few inches away from another person, another story, and you know that in the event of a crash, your skin will mingle with theirs. And then, these SNCF seats aren't comfortable. A little more room would be great. Room enough to stretch out and doze off, if you feel like it, all the way to the Gare de l'Est—and catch up on lost sleep. We're all trying to catch up on lost sleep. When you've got a neighbor, you have to sit up straight, almost like at school, and when the conductor goes by, you almost feel like raising a finger and saying, "Present."

But another side of me wants to protest. Why am I the only one without a temporary partner? Am I giving off the sort of body odor that immediately deters any hypothetical candidates? Am I that ugly? Do I frighten them? Intimidate them? So here I sit, the only person sitting alone in the whole car—isn't there even some old lady who could come and keep my thoughts from going round in circles? Or some vague acquaintance I could chat with about the weather or the passage of time?

I wonder what the other passengers think when they look at me. They see a woman who is neither young nor old, fairly well preserved. A somewhat inscrutable expression, lips that could stand to be a little fuller, a deep line across her forehead, two others on either side of her mouth. Light makeup. Nicely tailored clothes. Discreet elegance. Relatively slim figure. Why isn't she traveling first class?

For the simple reason that the 6:41 is a regional train, where the differences in comfort between first and second class are minimal. And besides, the number of first-class seats has been so drastically reduced that the half-car devoted to first is often jam-packed, while there are still empty seats in second class. Well, usually. Today the entire train is jammed. All that's left is the orphaned seat next to me. A privilege I would not have enjoyed in first class, where I would probably be stuck next to some corpulent senior executive reeking of aftershave, who would spend the entire time calling his superiors or his underlings, in spite of the notice requesting cell phones in sleep mode.

And besides, I like to travel second class. I feel like this is where I belong. My accountant laughs at me. He reminds me that *Pourpre et Lys* is one the trendiest shops around. That with two stores in Paris, one in Bordeaux, one in Lyon, and projects to expand all over France, I should start getting used to the idea that I have become an entrepreneur. Someone who in the decade ahead will count for something in the business world. In spite of the crisis, or because of it, organic beauty products have a bright future—particularly when the prices are still reasonable and the emphasis is placed on respect for regional traditions and on protecting the environment. Soaps that you cut yourself. Shampoo sold in reusable bottles. Ads printed on recycled paper. Clear, concise labels on plain brown paper, with the name of the product in black, and the ingredients below. Chic and sober. My brand.

Valentine and Luc have begun to realize. Luc increasingly shuts himself away in his study. A sort of rivalry has arisen between us and he's struggling, even though he's known from the start that he'll lose. Soon I'll be earning much more money than him.

He's been saying we have to move, we have to go back to Paris proper and leave our big house in the suburbs behind, the house with the garden where Valentine grew up. She couldn't care less either way. She's finishing her lycée and would rather stay with her friends for another year, but she's already informed me that she intends to have her own studio in a lively neighborhood right in Paris next year. The forty-five minute commute to Sucy, no thanks. Luc also thinks I should stop taking the RER now, but it's out of the question. My brand is also about reducing the executive personnel's expenditure. Even if I know that sooner or later we'll move back to the city; for the time being, the business is too precarious, and it could vanish in a puff of wind—poor management, competition, unrealistic ambitions. I don't want to add private loans to professional ones. At heart I'm still a provincial banker. After all, that's what I was trained to do. After two years of training in marketing techniques I found myself unemployed. So I got a vocational training certificate in banking. I pictured myself behind the counter in a branch in the town where I grew up. Sometimes life takes us a long way from the place we thought we were headed. Sometimes that's a good thing.

It has taken me quite awhile.

That's another of my character traits: I'm slow. But persevering. I thought about my project for years, when I was barely making ends meet as an administrative assistant in a financial analyst's office, then in one of those multinationals that are all about new technologies, cell phones, computers, and consoles. I sat there watching while those gung-ho reps crushed their competitors. Then witnessed their fall a few years later. I learned how to be discreet and impeccable to a fault. To be the model employee. To serve whoever was boss: the aging ones who couldn't keep up to speed and sat around dreaming of their retirement in the Sologne; the young ones who were working up to their first heart attack; they could be warm, icy, scathing, offhand. And I figured out how it all worked. I spent a lot of time reading, too. Books about business, accounting, marketing. Luc just laughed at me. He thought I was immersing myself in all that in order to get closer to him, to what he did every day. Because Luc is one of those aging, interchangeable, middle management execs—for a stationery company that is relocating by the hour. They don't even have a production site in France anymore. Hungary, Bulgaria, Poland: it's all concentrated in Eastern Europe.

Luc had his hour of glory when he was able to negotiate a schedule that would allow him to take Valentine to school every morning and pick her up in the evening, when she was small. He would chat with the other moms and with the primary school teachers. He was their darling, they were ecstatic to see a man looking after his kids. Those very same women who think it's only natural for the mother to do it—that's their role, after all, it's only fair. I hate women like them—because they are mainly women; they're the very reason clichés have such a long life.

And then, eight years ago now, everything changed. I came out with my plan. And I embellished it with an ultimatum to my husband: either you go along with it, or we split up. I let him call me every name in the book, but I knew he'd be there for me. Because he still loves me. Because he admires my combativeness. And because the project was unbeatable. The banks had already given their approval. The 2001 crisis was behind us, the 2008 crisis was still to come. And the banks felt like investing.

I have a good relationship with my husband.
Often difficult, but solid.
We're a team.
We know each other inside out; we are perfectly acquainted with each other's weaknesses and strengths. But we can still surprise one another. Last month, he suggested dropping everything in order to assist me if *Pourpre et Lys* really took off. That's the verb he used, "assist." With a smile, he pledged to be my vassal. I don't know many men who are capable of doing that.

Well, by the looks of it I'm going to sit here by myself. I really don't feel like consulting the latest figures or reading outstanding emails. I'll go back to the book I bought at the station on Friday on the way down. Some sort of family saga set in northern Germany. Nothing great, but it's restful. And that's what I need this morning, rest. I'm on my way home from the weekend and I'm exhausted. It's not a paradox. It's my life.

Ah-hah, there's a guy looking for somewhere to sit. He comes a bit closer. He stops. He glances at the seat. Hesitates. Keeps walking. Turns around again. I avoid looking at him. I can just detect his movement at the edge of my vision. For a moment I think I've won, that his desire for comfort is about to collide with the invisible wall of my indifference. No such luck. He clears his throat quietly, his voice is somewhat hoarse. "Excuse me, is this seat taken?" God, the idiotic phrases we say every day. I shake my head and sigh, just to let him know it really is a bother. I pull my bag out of the way and decide to look him in the face.

Oh. My. God.

Any more of my bullshit and I would have ended up standing for the entire trip—or sitting across from the toilets on one cheek.

Having said that, I did hesitate.

Because when I realized that the only seat available was next to Cécile Duffaut, I felt slightly dizzy, like the heroine of a nineteenth century novel, and I said to myself again, No, it can't be, and I thought I'd move on to the next car.

I'm almost positive she didn't recognize me. Because I'm hardly recognizable. The last time we spoke, it was twenty-six or twenty-seven years ago, something like that—downright prehistoric, and I wonder if I'd recognize myself if I ran into who I was back then. Last month when I was getting rid of stuff I came across some photos from back then, and I found it hard to "place" myself, so to speak. Let alone recover from the realization of how much I'd changed. I tend to forget that I haven't always had this beer belly—even though I'm no beer drinker—or that my hair is not so much brown as gray, and I have a marked tendency toward baldness, not to mention this overall flabbiness which reflects a complete lack of physical exercise.

She's changed, too, but—how to put it without getting annoyed—"for the better." That's it, she's changed for the better, because Cécile Duffaut was very ordinary back then and now look at her, she's a good-looking woman, as we say, and she doesn't look her age yet at all. Maybe a bit on the stern side, headmistressy, say, but really pretty. In fact, she is absolutely no more recognizable than I am, except that I've kept up with her transformation from a distance. Over the years I've spotted her from time to time in the center of town—I've been careful never to catch her eye, even crossing the road or changing my route. I went unnoticed. If she saw me, she never let on. I kept track of her career. And I heard about it, too. Through a woman I met after my divorce, and who went to lycée with us. This woman—Lucile? Lucie?—her parents and Cécile Duffaut's were friends. What I recall is that she's in business. Married. With one daughter. But that was a long time ago, so maybe it's all changed. Maybe she's gone through three divorces and she's a militant lesbian with eight adopted kids from Malawi and she's the head of an online company that promotes female wrestling.

In any case, she comes home on weekends sometimes to see her parents. The last time I spotted her must have been last year. She was with a tall, slim man. They were at the market, picking over the melons. Ain't life poetic, out in the provinces.

How awkward.

What are you supposed to do in this situation? Introduce yourself by saying something obvious like, "I think we've already met?" Or feign indifference and pretend to be surprised if the other person decides to make the first move: "Cécile Duffaut? I don't believe it!

I'm so sorry, I was completely absorbed in, well I mean I didn't ... well ... you understand ... that is ..." and make some vague gestures with your arms and hands, make the most of your pauses so that the other person can fill them with bursts of "Of course!" "Absolutely!" or "I can imagine!", all those expressions that serve no purpose, ever, I'm sick and tired of all those words that serve no purpose.

Or you can try the advanced Alzheimer's scenario, I really do not recognize you, you don't exist for me, you're just some meaningless neighbor on a meaningless train which is starting to pick up speed, why should I grant you anything more than a polite inattentiveness?

Right.

Here's what I'm going to do.

Act as if I don't know her—which is true, actually, we dated for three or four months twenty-seven years ago, what does that amount to? Nothing, nothing at all. She hasn't reacted, either. She doesn't remember me. So much the better, in the end. I have to keep one thing in mind: most people have a "delete" key which they will press at a given time, when their brain is about to overflow after all the misunderstandings and betrayals, all the hurt and disgrace—and when that happens, entire chunks of your existence disappear along with faces, names, addresses, colors, everything goes out the window into the sewers of the unconscious. I've got to remember that. Cécile Duffaut has obliterated everything. She went on with her life, and she is fine. Which is a relief. I can't see myself talking to her. It would be embarrassing. With

London and all that. So this is fine. I have other things to think about. More important than Cécile Duffaut.

Problems that affect me directly. That I have to come to grips with. My brain has to sort through all kinds of stuff.

There's Manon, for a start.

How can I explain to her that things won't last forever with this boy she's seeing? That she shouldn't go building castles in the air? That she shouldn't go thinking that once summer is over, with her in Reims and him back in Troyes, their relationship will manage to last? And so much the better, because he spends his time glued to his screen; he plans to study computer science, and a husband who's a geek is hardly the dream husband for your daughter. Or at least not for me. But if I start interfering in her love life, she'll get up on her high horse. She'll start talking about the divorce again. And my love life since then. And the fact that she's never criticized me. Then she'll add that as far as professions go, TV and stereo salesman doesn't exactly make for a dream dad, either.

Granted.

Keep my mouth shut.

That would be better.

And try to remember what it was like, when our parents used to butt into our love life.

Oh, my God.

My mother.

Whenever she met one of my girlfriends her face would split in two. The lower half was smiling, revealing her metal crown on the side, and she would chatter away, extremely pleasantly—too pleasantly, of course. With the upper half, she was examining, scrutinizing; a hard gaze searching for the slightest imperfection. And her eyebrows. That was what was most revealing: appreciation, disgust. I knew her body language by heart. It made me sick to my stomach.

And at dinner in the evening, her comments.

Or rather, her barbed arrows. Or how to stone someone with words. Comparisons. Better than the last one, not as good as the one before. I could picture the grades she was giving them in her mind. She had remained stuck on one of my first conquests, who wanted to become a schoolteacher, and for my mother, being a schoolteacher was the best possible job for a woman—it would ensure her of a certain independence, and it came with housing, and that was always a plus, and then above all teaching gave you the same vacation time as the children, which solved the problem of child care once and for all: "Don't go thinking I'll always be available to look after the children."

I remembered it well, that particular lesson. And she applied it from the moment Manon was born. Christine was a teacher. So we had no child care problems. Perfect. My mother could get on with her life with her bicycle salesman. She took it too far: I think Manon and Loïc only ever stayed overnight at her place—at their place—two or three times. My mother and her new guy were really mean to them, so as a result the kids never wanted to spend any time with their grandmother.

With parents, you have to make do with what you've got.

Let me think.

I wonder if Cécile Duffaut ever met my mother. No. I don't think she did. I was twenty when we were together. I was already studying at university. I had just moved into a studio in Paris, my aunt rented it to me for peanuts—a family favor. She warned me not to expect it to last forever. My cousins were starting the lycée, and they would want their independence soon enough. The apartment was so small it was impossible to imagine sharing the space.

I met Cécile Duffaut a few weeks after that. At a birthday party. To be honest, I don't know why I went out with her. Because I was bored, I suppose. Nothing to be proud of. Youth doesn't rule out stupidity. It lasted—how long? Three months? Four at the most. And even then, we only saw each other on weekends. I was living in Paris, she was in Troyes. It was nothing earth-shattering. Or even memorable. Except for the week in London. We took the train, one morning.

It's really weird to be in the same place twenty-seven years later. Not even speaking to each other. Maybe it's up to me to break the ice.

No.

This is ridiculous.

What would we talk about, for a start?

And besides, it's not talking I need.

It's thinking.

Sorting.

Done with Manon. Status quo.

Now on to Mathieu.

No, I don't need to think about Mathieu. I'm going to see him in a few hours. I'm going to look after him. The way I have already for two months. That's normal. I'm his best friend. Or at least I'm his friend. I was his best friend a long time ago. It's complicated. Now, he must have met Cécile Duffaut on two or three occasions. But he wasn't there on the night we began our affair. I think that if he'd been there, nothing would have happened. I wonder if he remembers her. I'll have to ask him later. At least it will be something to talk about. At times it can be a real lifesaver to have something trivial to talk about. Something light. That you can laugh about and elaborate on without arguing. Soap bubbles. What I'd like to do with Mathieu is blow soap bubbles. I could talk to him about the house, too. But Mathieu isn't interested in the house. That's a part of my life he knows nothing about. He never went there, when I was living with Christine. We weren't close at all. It was only after Christine and I split up that we got closer.

The house.

I've finally got a buyer. A builder who wants to gut it and restore "volume" to the rooms, which have a lot of "potential," but which feel "crushed by the color of the wallpaper." Builders talk now the way they do on those interior design programs on television. You'd think they're not masons or electricians anymore but interior decorators.

We have to talk about the price, but I already know that I'll come down. I'll be so glad to get rid of that place. I really wonder why after the divorce I ended up buying Christine's share. I said it was for the kids, so that they could always come and sleep in the place where they grew up. A grand illusion. First of all, because it was way too expensive for me on my own and I found myself up to my eyeballs in debt. And then, because they liked Jérôme's little house better—not so cluttered with furniture, more space, a big yard. And the prospect of a swimming pool. I should have gotten rid of it sooner, but it's like everything. I put things off. I procrastinate. The children left a long time ago and it's only this year that I decided to put the house on the market.

I don't know yet where I'll go. I'll rent something to start with. I might even, in the end, look for another job, or ask to be transferred. To the southwest, for example. What's keeping me here? My parents? They are mainly counting on my older brother to help them in their old age.

Yes.

Sell the house and move away. Good idea. An idea that brightens up the morning train, in any case. I can't help but smile. I almost feel like turning to Cécile Duffaut to start talking to her.

And that's what I would do if I weren't me.

Oh. My. God.

Philippe Leduc.

If only I had known.

I could change places. I'm one of those. The sort who can gather their belongings and stand up without saying a word, and who make sure they find peace and quiet for the rest of the trip at the other end of the train. In a restaurant, for example, I am capable of telling the waiter as he does his rounds to ask if everything is okay that, no, it's a disgrace, the food is disgusting, and I would like to see the chef so he can taste it himself. I am the epitome of the difficult customer.

But this time I can't. It's impossible. It's as if my feet were glued to the floor. I'm a tin soldier. It's incredible. As if I were a teenager all over again. And it annoys me. Especially as I had planned to sink into the novel and enjoy the ride from Troyes to Paris as a sort of interlude, a long deep breath of fresh air before the turmoil of the week ahead.

It's unbearable.

What I feel now is pure hatred. And that surprises me—because I'm not like that, particularly toward someone I haven't seen in what must be at least twenty-five years. Twenty-seven, in fact. I can't help but sneak looks at him. His profile. His build. My God. It's incredible. He doesn't look at all like he used to.

Because although you might not think so, I still have a fairly precise memory of his features. Which is odd, because there are entire chunks of my life that I hardly remember, there are people who have mattered far more than Philippe Leduc, but I can't remember their faces, whereas his I can see perfectly well. If I close my eyes—at the party, at the edge of the garden. Or in the loft, afterward. In a hotel room in London. They're like snapshots. I have to get rid of them.

Then I open my eyes and turn my head slightly to the right—what a disaster. He is unrecognizable. Old, for a start. Wrinkled. Flabby. With sagging shoulders. A definite paunch. A scraggly beard. The kind of man who, above all else, inspires pity. Yes, that's it exactly.

Well, well.

If I had known that one day I would feel pity where Philippe Leduc is concerned, I would have laughed out loud. Hatred, yes. But pity mingled with compassion, certainly not. If someone could have told me that's how I would feel, it would have done me a world of good. When you break up with someone, you ought to be able to foresee even ever so briefly what the other person will be like years from now. In three cases out of four, you would stop weeping and feeling sorry for yourself. You'd laugh, and it would do you a world of good. Although I didn't go around feeling sorry for myself. It was all a kind of a blank afterward. My feelings went numb. Into a fog. A redefinition of roles. And on the train taking me back to France, that sudden surge of hatred. A voracious feeling inside, the likes of which I had never known. A desire to tear everything to shreds.

And that's what's welling up in me now—but it's not intact. Because it has been confronted with that slumping figure—what happened to all that brio he once had? My hatred is waning. It's tinged with scorn.

Philippe Leduc.

If you only knew.

The last time I thought about Philippe Leduc, I had just met Luc. We were in his studio in the 18th arrondissement, at Lamarck-Caulaincourt, getting in each other's way. We loved it. We had just spent the weekend by the Somme Bay. We were beginning to think that maybe living together, dot, dot, dot … And we'd finish the sentence in silence, each in our own fashion. Luc must have thought that I was replacing the dot, dot, dot … with a blue sky filled with white clouds, happy toddlers, and blissful motherhood—to be honest, there was some of that, but not only. There was, above all, a girl walking straight ahead and casting an ironic and somewhat cruel gaze at everything around her. Though I would never have admitted such a thing, obviously.

We were on the highway. Luc had his eyes closed. On the radio, they were playing Dionne Warwick's "Heartbreaker" and suddenly I was back in London. Summertime London, with the windows open, the yellowed grass in the gardens and parks; it had been hot, very hot, it wasn't like England at all, enlightened scientists were proclaiming that this was the beginning of global warming, the end of the human race, Armageddon. I walked through those London streets at night, and the paths I would take in the future were being traced. A London that Philippe Leduc had ruined forever. I knew I would never go back there because of all the sickening memories, and that's what made me angrier than anything—to realize that a place I had liked was now off-limits. I have never been back. I have suppliers in Great Britain, of course—after all, that's where the idea for the shops came from—but I have entrusted Amy to handle the business with them because she's a native speaker, it's only natural.

In the car that day I saw Luc's profile and the shape of my life to come. Although in all that time I hadn't given much thought to Philippe Leduc, because the images disgusted me, in the car that day I faced him, mentally. And I was neither as straight nor as sharp as I would have liked to be. Because a part of me wondered what had become of him and whether he ever looked at himself in the mirror and thought about London. And that same part of me was convinced that it had been a terrible waste. That in fact we could have gotten along. That he could have been sitting there where Luc was. That the men I met were interchangeable.

The very idea was horrifying.

I swept it away with the back of my hand, and Luc opened his eyes. He asked me what was wrong. I mumbled, "Nothing, I'm just feeling kind of sad, that's all." We pulled off at the next rest area and he took the wheel.

Now it makes me laugh.

I'm looking at Philippe Leduc out of the corner of my eye. I'm getting used to his new physique. The fact I recognized him right away must mean he hasn't changed all that much. But for sure he has gone downhill. He looks drab. What was so attractive back then was that spark he had. Not just in his eyes, but in the way he moved. The way he laughed. The velvet texture of his skin. You told yourself that with a guy like that life would be one endless party. I don't know where he got it—the absence of misfortune, perhaps. He was someone who at the age of twenty had never had any reason to complain. He was good-looking, his parents indulged his every whim, his brother was a good deal older than him and already out of his way, and he had more friends than you could ever hope for. No rough edges. No scrapes or scratches. There are people like that, who seemed to float their way through the years, and then along comes a first emotional or professional disappointment, or the death of a friend or a family member, and everything shatters.

He looks pretty shattered to me.

He was very popular at the lycée, Philippe Leduc. We weren't in the same class, but I'd noticed him. Some of the girls in my clique would talk about him. Their comments were by no means all positive. Particularly on the part of a redhead who'd gone out with him: a total fiasco, she said. She shouted out for all to hear that he was despicable. We nodded, but deep down we thought she spoke that way out of bitterness. We were sure that with us it would be different.

I was only in the outer circle of that group. I never viewed Philippe Leduc as potential prey. I had no potential prey. I was realistic. I wasn't all that attractive, I had brown hair that got greasy overnight and defied all my efforts to control it. An ordinary face. I didn't make any effort, either. I had no desire to look pretty. I'd gone out with two boys you could refer to as lumps: losers of my own caliber. I parted with my virginity without too much pain but also without any pleasure.

I don't have any good memories of the lycée. It was only afterward that I made real friendships. Along the way, two years after I'd finished, there was Philippe Leduc.

The last image I have of him. That angelic little mug of his: I felt like blowing it to smithereens. My entire body full of tension in the effort to seem calm. And snapshots from the previous days: the rope bracelet he wore on his left wrist. The fine muscles on his arms. His thighs. His butt. I can still see it all quite sharply. I'm biting my lips not to laugh. If he only knew, Philippe Leduc, how I am eyeing his butt from twenty-seven years ago, it'd blow his mind. I'm starting to talk like Valentine.

I don't want to imagine what his butt is like nowadays. I'll bet it's succumbed to the same fate as all the rest—sagging. Lassitude. I wish I could see myself in the mirror. To see whether I'm a similar disaster area.

That's what I did the day after the party we went to together. I can just picture myself. Naked in the bathroom. Inspecting every feature, mercilessly. I couldn't understand what he saw in me. Because I was perfectly realistic. When I was at the lycée, the girls there had really helped me. They thought I was plain. Not ugly, no, just plain. Nothing striking. A bug. I knew he'd had a lot to drink by the time we started talking out in the garden. That when we sought refuge in the attic, away from the others, he had alcohol in his blood. We thought it would be full of cobwebs and old toys and wardrobes stuffed with cast-off clothes, but what we found was a regular two-room apartment, with a bed and armchairs and a coffee table. We stood there for a moment, astonished. He was holding my hand. We wondered whether we dared violate this space that didn't belong to us or even to the boy who had invited us, but to his parents. It was as if we had walked straight into adulthood.

And violate we did.

That next day as I stood at the mirror in the bathroom, I kept my emotions in check. I told myself I'd been very lucky. But I shouldn't get my hopes up. He wouldn't call. It would be better if I forgot about him. And that was still my strategy when he came up to me the following Friday as I was on my way out of the technical institute. He wanted to talk to me. To apologize. For what had happened last week. I lifted my chin. I said, "Don't worry about it. I wanted to. And anyway, I've forgotten all about it." He was stunned. No one spoke to Philippe Leduc like that. He went on the attack. I'd nailed him. I hadn't planned it. It would never have worked if I had. He took me by the arm. I turned to look at him. I was very solemn. I studied his face. I dissected him the way we dissected the company reports we worked on in our business classes.

He was the one who melted first.

We became an item—sort of.

I say sort of. Because apart from during vacations, we met only on weekends. I went to two or three parties in Paris that his friends from university threw. I stayed in the background. He was ingratiating. A lot of people wondered what we were doing together, but at the same time they didn't really ask questions, and in any case, when you're twenty, couples come and go. Before long we would be ancient history, too.

He was the one who wanted to go to London.

I remember how it came about. We were at the café, Les Trois Amis, not far from my parents' place. I went past the place just this weekend, when I took my mother to the boulangerie that isn't a boulangerie. It hasn't changed. The same wrought iron tables outside, the same little gravel courtyard. The veranda has been painted green. You can just get a glimpse of the room at the back, a bit too dark. My mother followed my gaze. She delighted in telling me that the owners had recently put the café on the market, because they were about to retire. I waited for her to go on, to start annoying me and say how she hoped that this den of iniquity, of debauched youth, would be wiped from the surface of the planet, because there had always been problems, with noise and concerts and drunken customers, but she merely gave a little sigh and said she hoped the new owners would keep it as a bar. "It's a good thing, it livens up the neighborhood, it's fun to see all these young people." I couldn't believe my ears. My mother used to hate it when I hung out at Les Trois Amis.

I thought about old age. About change. About the boredom of repetition.

Maybe I'll tell her that I was on the train with Philippe Leduc.

No.

She wouldn't remember him. She saw him only two or three times.

And yet he made a huge impression on her. She thought, Well I never, for once Cécile has brought home an attractive young man. Who's got presence. And manners on top of it. It's true that Philippe was the perfect son-in-law. Smiling, relaxed, considerate toward older people, opening the car door for the ladies, well-mannered. He was studying English, the language of the future, but he didn't brag about his abilities. He made friends wherever he went. He was the young man at family reunions who tickles the kids and makes the grandmothers laugh.

I thought he took it too far.

I knew what made me want to be with him: vanity. To parade around on the arm of a handsome man. To show other people that even when you're insignificant you can still manage to do such a thing. I was perfectly aware that the relationship wasn't headed anywhere and that it would end soon enough. But not the way it did. No, not like that.

I'm sure my mother also wondered what miracle had propelled us into each other's arms—even if it was only for a few months.

Sex. That's what I should have told her, just to see her face. And because it was part of the explanation. To him, I was reassuring.

In bed, Philippe Leduc was no longer quite so high and mighty. He was clumsy. More than once it was a near fiasco. And he was uptight, as well. He simply could not walk around naked. I never found out why he was like that. There was a time when I would have thought it could be interesting to get to the bottom of it, but we weren't close enough for that. And then later on it no longer mattered anyway.

But I liked to reassure him. I would cling to his back without saying anything. I knew that talking would be the worst thing. So I would put my hand between his thighs and my lips on his shoulder blades and stay there without moving. I closed my eyes. I tried to imagine everything that was going through his mind—bits of conversations, locker room bragging, clips from porn films, and other dream-like sequences of drownings or fires or railroad disasters. And then very gradually the calm would return. Memories of a deep blue lake in the mountains. Walking along the ocean. Slowly, beneath my fingers, he would regain his vigor. I know that he liked this about me. My discretion. My patience. Then I would take over, still ever so gently. That's what he needed, gentleness. That's why our affair lasted for months and not days. That's also why I was so angry with him afterward.

What am I doing?

Now I can see my hand on his dick, very clearly, twenty-seven years ago. And yet there he is right next to me and I'm pretending not to recognize him. It's unbelievable, sometimes, the sudden turns life can take. It feels good to have that perspective. I'd rather not face him, confront what he has become. I'd rather stay where I am with the colorful impression of his young body. With my head against the dirty windowpane of the train car. Do not disturb, I'm asleep. It feels gentle. So incredibly gentle.

London. It's only normal that I would think about London. The first time I went there was with Cécile Duffaut. I had my discount from the railway, and she'd worked for them, too, the summer before we met, and she'd hardly spent a thing. That was her all over. Thrifty. Everything in moderation. Values you aren't supposed to appreciate when you're only twenty—they only gradually turn into values. I still admire people who can blow their entire salary at a casino in one night, or who give up everything to start all over on the other side of the planet. Except that now I know I've never been one of those people.

I think I was the one who first mentioned London. I was studying English, but I'd never set foot in England, not even the year I was thirteen for the three-day school trip: two days before we were due to leave I twisted my ankle during basketball practice, and I was left behind, frustrated as hell.

She said yes right away. A discreet little yes, her eyes glued to her shoes, but a definite yes all the same. I remember I was surprised. I thought she'd be one of those girls who'd rather go visiting villages in the Corrèze or the wilds of Provence so they'd be alone with their sweetheart. She added that travel was vitally important to her. So she could broaden her horizons. And take a breather. I listened to her and thought how she was full of surprises.

We were growing up in an era when flying was still the exception, and to wake up in New York or Tokyo would have seemed beyond our reach. Computers were at the experimental stage, and no one could imagine that one day we would no longer need phone booths. On the other hand, the future seemed wide open, and the planet, eternal.

She told me she would like to go to London, too, so we started planning. It was strange to be planning a trip for a whole week with a girl I intended to dump. But it wouldn't be the first time I'd behaved inconsistently. And the thing that was disturbing about her was that every time I decided I'd tell her enough was enough, she would sidestep me in a way that revealed some hidden part of her personality. She was unpredictable. And that wasn't a quality I had often encountered. She might be ordinary, but she had nerve. It was refreshing.

It's horrible to rationalize like this. I've never claimed to be an angel. But I do hope I've improved over time.

There's less room for surprise when you're forty-seven. You're caught up in a daily grind, a life beyond your control: relationships, divorce, children, work, social life, responsibilities. Only insomnia occasionally sets you free, by revealing the futility of everything you've undertaken. But I'm speaking for myself. I don't know what sort of life she has. Other than that she visits her parents from time to time and that to go home she takes the 6:41 train.

London lingers.
The London from back then. The early '80s. Noth-

ing very inspiring. The punk era was over, Thatcherism was changing mentalities but hadn't yet changed the life in the streets, the city was neither here nor there. It was neither the swinging London of the '60s nor the business and finance showcase it would later become. It was looking for an identity. Maybe that's why I felt so good there. I used to love London. I saw a documentary last year about the new neighborhoods along the Thames: I didn't recognize a thing.

Cécile Duffaut's knee.

There it is again, suddenly.

On a double-decker bus.

We are on the top deck. You can still smoke, on the top deck. The sun, relentlessly beating down on the city. We're somewhere north of Regent's Park, headed toward Primrose Hill. We're on our way back from Camden. She's leaning her forehead on the window. She's totally absorbed by the streets, the buildings, the taxis, the bustle.

All I can see is her knee.

Her knee, peeking out from under a red skirt. It's not a woman's knee. It's a little girl's knee, and it's easy to picture it with scrapes and Mercurochrome and Band-Aids. The kind of knee that has a special acquaintance with gravel, blacktop, and the curb of the sidewalk. A graceless knee. I'm getting annoyed with this knee. It is a distillation of everything I hate about her: her ordinariness, her lack of polish or refinement. The fact that I feel guilty makes me all the more irritated. I know I've been behaving badly over the last few days.

This little girl with scraped knees: I'm ruining her life. Her memories. In advance. I'm mad at myself. And the madder I get, the more sure of myself I get. We have to break up. We should have done it a long time ago. I don't know what came over me. In my memory, her knee is ugly. Lumpy. Knobbly. I wonder what it's really like.

And now?

I should ask her to show me her knees.

What the hell is wrong with me?

I have to stop thinking about all this stuff. And anyway, she's asleep, in the same position as on the bus in London. She looks tired. I'll bet her weekends with her parents are no picnic. I hardly ever see my mother and her bicycle salesman. They're always gallivanting about. They belong to that generation I've begun to despise. The baby boomers who never really knew any hardship. Scarcely any memories of the war—they were born in the middle of it or just afterward, and they grew up with their faith in the evolution of capitalism, an improved standard of living, comfort and health care, and full employment. Together they were marching in step toward a radiant future made of washing machines and refrigerators. A little bit too old for the unrest in 1968, but they welcomed the cultural and sexual revolutions with open arms. They had their apartment, then their little house, retirement at sixty, a long life expectancy, they have their savings accounts, and now their kids are out of the house and they fly all over the planet and so what if they are destroying the environment. They know everything will go on getting worse after they're gone—

and they don't give a damn.

My mother and Cycleman spend their weekends in Barcelona or Venice. They sign up for cruises and play Scrabble while they listen to some band playing their favorite hits from the 1960s. They take bus tours to Eastern Europe and exclaim, Oh, how hard it must have been for the East Germans, the Czechs, the Slovaks, the Lithuanians, oh my God, how awful, can you imagine— and then they go back to their bargain luxury hotel for dinner and complain because the staff don't speak French.

I hardly ever see them. The last I heard, Cycleman bought a motorcycle—now that's a revolution. They're planning their first trip with their new vehicle, and they can't make up their minds: Collioure or the Aquitaine?

I can see Mathieu's back, as if it were yesterday. We're eighteen years old, almost nineteen. The two of us on his motorcycle. His parents just bought it for him, secondhand. I'm insanely jealous ... as far as two-wheeled vehicles go, I've never progressed any further than the metallic blue Peugeot 103 SP moped that got stolen after only two months, and which my parents refuse to replace. "You'll just have to use your dad's old Solex moped instead." Mathieu is driving fast. He'll be going to Germany for his military service soon. He dropped out of school. He doesn't know what to do in life. He's been thinking of acting, but everyone keeps telling him it's not really a profession. And recently an amateur theater director told him he didn't have the looks for the job. He's too pudgy. Too heavy. He's at a complete loss. It's fall. We're getting lost down country roads, Mathieu and me. It's an interlude. Nothing seems to matter anymore. I guess that when he comes back from Germany we'll already be headed in different directions. This is probably the last time we'll be this close. I'm convinced that something will happen—a puddle of oil, a truck inching into our lane, a collision, a violent crash and then—blackout.

Nothing of the sort.

Of course not.

No one ever warned us that life would be long.

Those easy slogans that make your heart beat faster, like "carpe diem" or "die young"—all that stuff was just nonsense.

No one told us, either, that the hardest thing would not be breaking up, but decay. The disintegration of relationships, people, tastes, bodies, desire. Until you reach a sort of morass where you no longer know what it is you love. Or hate. And it's not as unpleasant a condition as you might think. It's just lifelessness. With scattered spots of light. One of them is going to see Mathieu this morning, after so much time has elapsed.

Ah-hah, Cécile Duffaut is sitting up.

Had a bad night, huh?

I know what she must be going through. Life is full of bad nights, once you turn forty. Your children's health, your own, their future, your own, the litany of work still to be done on the house, the electricity which still needs childproofing, the toilets have been leaking for three months, the vacation rental needs booking, how do you clean the spots made by permanent markers from the table in the living room, the car is making a strange noise when it's in neutral, above all don't forget to get gas tomorrow morning otherwise you're sure to run out, I haven't read a novel in ages, even though it's something I used to love, reading novels, I have to fill out the forms for my younger boy's upcoming school trip, lists, lists, lists, they start filling your nights—you get up, you go down the stairs, it's three o'clock in the morning, you bump into the furniture, you shiver, you think about making a coffee but what sort of crazy idea is that, a coffee at this time of night, so you go for a citrus herbal tea, you switch on the electric kettle, see your reflection in the mirror with the kettle in one hand and the citrus tea bag in the other, you hardly know who that person is.

But when Cécile Duffaut looks at herself in the mirror, her reflection must give her a bit more of a boost, after all. When we were dating, I'm sure people pictured what we'd be like later on: she'd be a crotchety old maid and I'd be the philandering husband type, with three divorces behind me, but still in great shape. It's mind-boggling when you find out how little you really know. When I was with Cécile Duffaut, I …

Just the thought of it, "When I was with Cécile Duffaut": how weird is that.

This is ridiculous. I should introduce myself to her.

Oh, here comes the conductor.

It's times like this that I realize how far I still have to go—and given my age, I'll probably never get that far.

Normally, a businesswoman like me, at the age of forty-seven, would be traveling first class and then, when the conductor came, she would discreetly and efficiently open her handbag and take out her ticket—which would be tucked away in a neat little compartment designed specifically for that purpose.

But we're dealing with me here, me and those character traits I haven't managed to get rid of, and which I try to accommodate as best I can.

I empty out practically my entire handbag onto the tray—I can see the conductor's mocking smile and worse still, Philippe Leduc's. I can imagine the typical comments going through their minds, about women's handbags, and how we seem to need to carry our entire lives around in such a little thing.

I keep on looking.

I try to maintain my dignity, to search methodically, with a detached and scornful manner. Above all without blushing or babbling. Without making up one excuse after the other, or telling stories. It's an embarrassing moment. The conductor doesn't want to rush me, so he pretends to be gazing around the railroad car, as if some extremely important event were unfolding in the vicinity of the toilets. Philippe Leduc turns his head to the right and acts absorbed in the monotonous landscape. We have just gone through Romilly-sur-Seine. And I wonder if he remembers the evening we spent there when we were together. I had friends who lived there, and they threw a party. We took the train. At one point we left the smoke-filled house and wandered through the deserted streets—along the endless wall that runs down the main street. I said, "One thing's for sure, I'll never live here." He answered with a cliché, about how there was no way we could ever know what the future held in store. I rolled my eyes, and I remember that because of his remark all of a sudden he went down a notch in my esteem. *Could do better. Must work on repartee. Try to shine in ways other than good looks alone. Make an effort.* That was what I felt like saying. But of course nothing came out.

At the same time, stereotypes die hard, and above all, they do contain an element of truth. How could we have foreseen that over a quarter of a century later we would go through that town again, sitting side by side, pretending not to know each other?

In the meantime, the conductor is waiting.

I take a deep breath.

I will not allow myself to be intimidated. I've changed. I'm a woman who is in charge. Who is sure of herself and of her choices.

And anyway, there it is, the ticket.

There are some habits you never lose. I think that if you'd mentioned Cécile Duffaut to me before this morning, the first thing that would have sprung to mind was the way she had to empty out her handbag every time she had to find something: a pack of chewing gum, cigarettes, a phone number, a checkbook. Or a train ticket. It's reassuring. This loyalty to who you really are, in spite of everything. In spite of the elegant clothes which must have cost a fortune. In spite of her looks, far more attractive than in the old days.

I wonder what defines me, now. What characteristics I had already ten, fifteen, or twenty years ago, and that I didn't try to do anything about.

Like separating the soft part of the bread from the crust and rolling it into tiny balls, while continuing to talk with someone, who would be transfixed, even concerned: he's not going to go and eat those things, is he? Oh yes he is.

Like making sure the alarm on the clock radio is set at the right time, checking four times in a row, otherwise I have to start all over. In another life, I must have had many obsessive-compulsive behaviors; in this life, that's the only one I have.

Staring at the ceiling whenever I start feeling emotional; keeping my eyes glued to the paint, the color, the cracks.

Scattering coins all over the place whenever I get undressed—they go springing from my pockets and rolling across parquet floors, waking everyone in the house. It's easier now that I'm alone at night. I could never stand the idea of a wallet, that lump in your pocket. It used to drive Christine crazy. I suppose that Jérôme knows how to behave. Or only carries bills. That are ironed. He knows how to get undressed with grace and dignity. Those are two words I'm not too familiar with, grace and dignity. For a while I enjoyed the illusion of self-confidence that comes with the energy of youth, but then it was gone.

I'm on edge.

From sensing her sitting there next to me. In fact, I ought to change seats. Pretend to get off at the next station. Except that the train is nonstop from Troyes to Paris. But why do I need to give any explanation? I don't owe Cécile Duffaut anything. I am nothing to her, she is nothing to me, and that's all there is to it. So why do I stay? Guilt? A little, I suppose. In hopes that she might speak to me? Pathetic. Laziness?

I wonder what she remembers. Well, that is, what she would remember if she had recognized me.

Going for drives in the Peugeot 204. I paid next to nothing for that car. It was white. The same one my parents had when I was a kid. I liked having the gear stick at the wheel. The seats still smelled of leather after all those years. Cécile didn't have her license yet. We weren't going anywhere in particular. We were wasting gas. We smoked, with the windows cracked open.

The Peugeot 204 was my revenge for Mathieu's

motorcycle. As I thought, I saw less of Mathieu after he came back from Germany. And when we got together he would always say how lucky I was to have a car. He had become a regular on the train, the RER, and the Métro; he kept going up to Paris to try his luck. He was having a hard time. Sleeping on friends' sofas, on mattresses on the floor, sometimes right on the floor. Sleeping out on the street, too, on those occasions when he didn't manage to sponge off someone. He was losing his cheerful nature. I'm not really sure when things began to change for him. At one point, he almost disappeared from sight, but then when he reappeared he had landed himself a supporting role in a TV movie. But he refused to talk about it. Then another long spell of silence. He had plunged into another world. I missed him. Even though I was struggling with my own demons, and the desire to make my own way in life, I missed him. I could have asked his parents for news. I was too proud. When I got my first real contract, at the superstore where I still work, he was the one I wanted to call before anyone else. But to tell him what? To brag about how now I was qualified to sell TVs and VCRs? I didn't want to hear myself telling him that. Even though I knew that this job was a lifesaver, since I'd given up studying English, and gone back to the town where I was born, and spent months looking for work; even after all the broken promises. No. I figured I'd call him when I found something else.

After that, I worked on other friendships. There were colleagues. Christine. Christine's friends. That was it.

Sometimes just as I was falling asleep I would think about Mathieu. I wondered what he was doing. I'd had news of him indirectly. I watched the TV movies he played in. And the feature films, where his tall, slender physique was becoming more and more visible. That was what surprised me more than anything: I had always thought of Mathieu as plump. The guy whose screen career I was vaguely following didn't look anything like him. Even his voice seemed to have changed. It was deeper.

Whenever I came out of the movie theater, I felt like calling him—and I never got up the resolve.

The only consolation in all those years was my family. Christine. The girls. I waited anxiously for the day when Mathieu's photo would appear in some celebrity magazine with a gorgeous Spanish actress or Ukrainian supermodel on his arm, and the cryptic caption underneath: "Could that little bulge at the waist be the sign of an future joyful event?"

It never happened.

First of all because his love affairs never lasted very long. But above all because he never became famous. For a long time he was a familiar face, but in the background. His career would have been completely lackluster had it not been for *Today's Lucky Winners*. *Today's Lucky Winners* was really a stroke of luck for him. He was well acquainted with the producer of the program, who was looking for an experienced host not too well-known to the general public. They did some screen tests. Bingo. There he was in one of the most popular programs on French television: a pathetic game show, perfect for filling the lonely hours of the unemployed or housewives under fifty, while they wait for the one o'clock news. His sense of humor, his handsome face, his easy way with people: in a few weeks, he walked off with the jackpot. Money was no longer a problem. It was 2004; he was forty years old. His future was all sewn up.

It was around then that Christine and I got divorced. It was also around then that I stopped buying the *TV Guide*. I couldn't stand seeing pictures of Mathieu anymore. I was only too aware of how our paths in life were heading in different directions. We had met at a time when he was merely a rough draft of the person he would later become, while I was at my zenith. He would keep on rising, whereas I had begun to sink gradually. Every time I caught his face in a magazine, those were my thoughts. About failure. About destiny slipping out of your grasp.

I'm better now.

And I'm on my way to visit Mathieu today.

Gulp.

I'm not proud of myself.

And I know why.

He's the one who got back in touch. I would never have dared. Not because I would have been afraid of disturbing him. But because I was afraid of being humiliated: What if he could hardly remember my name?

I ran into his mother, just after my divorce. She was shopping at the store. She wanted to buy a new television.

She had just lost her husband—I hadn't heard about it. We spoke for a long time. She invited me over for the following Sunday, a Sunday when I didn't have the kids. She'd bake a cake. When I left the store that evening, I felt like crying—as much over her solitude as over the way my life was going. I was going to be filling in for my erstwhile best friend. He had dreamed of being in my place; now I was taking his. I was stepping into the shoes of the man he might have been, the lonely man who visits his mother for Sunday tea.

One day, Mathieu found out. I thought it would make him angry. It was worse than that. He felt pity. And it's true, basically, that pity was all I deserved—a fortysomething guy taking refuge at the home of his childhood friend's mother, talking about life, how lame can you get. But I liked going to Maud's place. Peeling vegetables with her. Doing the sort of daily activities I had never done with my parents. What I liked was that Maud wasn't judgmental. Even less so nowadays that she's been diagnosed with Alzheimer's. I look back on those days and really miss them, almost more than any other time in my life. My dinners at Maud's. My Sundays spent preparing tasty dishes while exchanging thoughts about life, neighbors, children. I miss her.

Mathieu and I started calling each other because of her. I had just found her in the parking lot of the store, distraught and completely disoriented. I called the doctor. Then her son. I remember Mathieu's voice on the telephone. And the voice he had as an adolescent. Nothing remotely like the grave, confident timbre he'd created for his TV movies. Nor like the exaggeratedly cheerful self he'd adopted for *Today's Lucky Winners*. Truth be told, he wasn't very lucky that day. He had to rely on me. To ask me a favor. Maybe the first of many. He was beholden to me.

That's how we became friends once again.

Friends.

That's saying a lot.

Let's just say that it was saying a lot until recently. We would call each other. He would stop by from time to time. We only talked about his mother and his career. One day he did ask me, however, if it hadn't been too rough on me, the divorce. In fact, I'd been through it already long before, so I was able to smile and shrug and say, "That's life." I don't know why, but it must have touched him, so he invited me to his place. In Paris. To his apartment. To a party with his Parisian friends.

It was an honor.

There I was in that milieu where I didn't belong, among people who drank too much and laughed very loudly, among tired-but-bubbly wives, and catering staff who walked around with finger food and refills. Mathieu simply introduced me as, "Philippe, a childhood friend." They all stared at me with a big smile for ten seconds or so and then the conversation would continue, without me. I melted into the décor. It wasn't hard. I felt like I was in a bad TV movie. I recognized a few faces I'd spotted on the TV screen, but I couldn't put a name on any of them. The big shots had promised they'd come but at the last minute they called to cancel. Or didn't call. And Mathieu really didn't mind at all. What was radiant about Mathieu's place was Mathieu himself.

Also radiant that evening was a woman twenty years younger than him, lively and witty. Who worked as an usher at a theater to pay for law school. Totally on top of things. Her name was Astrid. Even at the very heart of the party she was true to herself. She would drift toward Mathieu and then away again, perfectly natural and nonchalant. I envied her. I envied Mathieu, too, of course. They'd been seeing each other for a few months, but she had no illusions. Sooner or later their affair would end, she would get tired of playing the gerontophile or he would find a woman who was more docile.

At one point the volume went up a notch, and she and I ended up in the huge kitchen. The caterer and his assistants had left, they'd be back in the morning to clean up. It was very late. She found a bunch of black grapes, and began to eat them one by one.

"You know, Mathieu often speaks of you."

"Oh. In flattering terms, I hope."

"I wouldn't know. At the same time, it's fairly recent. Out of the blue."

"Blue moon. As in, once in—that's how often we've seen each other."

I tried to change the subject. I got the feeling it was headed in a direction that might prove unpleasant.

"It's because I was looking after his mother."

"Or his mother was looking after you. Well, that's how he put it."

"Sometimes human relations go both ways."

"For a while, people were making fun of you around here. All these people you see here, they'd slap their hands on their thighs whenever they heard one of Mathieu's stories about Philippe making apple pie with his friend's mom."

"I'm not sure I really want to hear this."

"Wait. It's not as bad as it sounds. And in life, truth is the greatest asset, don't you think?"

I imagined getting to my feet with dignity—it wouldn't be hard, I had drunk only two glasses of champagne. Something had prevented me from drinking more—the fear of making a slip, of feeling nauseous, of making a fool of myself. I imagined walking across the kitchen and through the crowd in the living room, picking up my coat, going down the stairs and, whistling, making my way to the Gare de l'Est, where the first trains would soon be departing. I imagined disappearing.

Yes, I saw myself doing all that, but I am an actor only in my dreams. In reality, I nodded and poured myself a glass of water.

"Gradually it changed. You became a … what should I call it, yes, a kind of character witness. He refers to you as if you were a character witness."

"I beg your pardon?"

"He's come in for quite a lot of criticism lately. Let's just say that he behaved badly with certain individuals. And people began saying that he was forgetting where he was from, that he was getting bigheaded. He had to get things back on an even keel. He was antagonizing everyone. So he did a lot of soul-searching. And you are part of that. You allow him to show that no, he hasn't changed. That he's had the same friends for years. That he's stayed close to his roots. That the things he was being accused of were unjustified."

I poured myself some strong booze. Over ice. I swirled the ice cubes in the glass. None of this came as a surprise. What did astonish me, however, was that I didn't feel more offended. I was past all that. I shrugged.

"I'm sorry if this comes as a blow," she said.

"I'm past feeling any blows. I'm already on the ground."

"I like you a lot, you know."

"Do you need a character witness as well?"

I looked up at her from under my brows. For a moment she didn't know what to say, then she burst out laughing.

"What are you going to do with it?"

"With what?"

"With what I've just told you."

"Nothing at all. He's taking advantage of the situation. So am I. It's not exactly as if I'm swamped with invitations. And then when I get home and go into work I can always casually mention the fact that I spent an evening with Mathieu Coché. Everyone finds their misplaced vanity where they can."

"I don't know why I spoke to you about truth just now. You don't need any lessons from me."

"On the other hand, I would like a refill."

On we went like that, in the kitchen, just the two of us. Words whizzing by. Minutes, too. This hadn't happened to me in a long time. I think we confided in each other the way people rarely confide in each other. We knew perfectly well that we would never meet again. That one of us was bound to be exiting Mathieu's life before long. I was prepared to go away again, the way I had come. But in the end she was the one who slammed the door—which meant that I got to stay on and put up with Mathieu ranting and raving against women. Particularly younger women. Before we left the kitchen, early that morning, after the party, we exchanged phone numbers. To be used only in case of an urgent need to confide—which meant never. I still have her number on me, in my wallet. It has become a sort of talisman. I could call her now and tell her about Cécile. About Mathieu. About the nagging reluctance I feel going to see Mathieu.

Dear God, what am I doing on this train?

Next to Cécile.

Who suddenly stands up.

And brushes past my knees.

"Sorry."
"No problem."
"Excuse me."
"Of course."

I'm in the toilet, checking my face in the mirror. My cheeks are red. I am being ridiculous. Why is my heart pounding as if it's about to burst? Because I just exchanged two polite but awkward phrases with a fellow passenger on the train? Because I brushed against the knee of a man who is neither young nor old, who has a paunch and an incipient bald patch? It's nothing to get in such a state about. Because ... just take a look. Take a good look at yourself in the mirror. Look at me.

You're a hundred times better than he is.

Only a faint touch of makeup. Your skin, still glowing thanks to a simple night cream. Your eyes, with just a hint of liner. You're a walking advertisement for the products you sell: you're radiant, in spite of the years creeping up on you. And your hair. You even have trouble taming your hair, it still grows wild, with a late-blooming vitality.

You're a hundred times better than he is.

Men. There are those who look at you during meetings. And those who like your efficiency and relative discretion. Some of them would like to know what you're hiding behind that calm veneer. Others tremble when your decisions are final. There are those who, on public transport, take a good look at you and compare you with the woman they will go home to when they come to their stop. Some of them will sigh because of the comparison. Others would like to go up to you but don't dare, because, though you'd never know it, there's a side to you that's intimidating.

Then there is Luc, of course. Months, years of struggle just to keep his attention, to feel his growing admiration, to ward off all those women who thought they could come and unravel the close-knit family unit you've been creating. So different from the one you grew up in. So far removed, mentally, that you almost never tell your parents about your everyday life anymore. Because they wouldn't understand; they can't even begin to picture it.

I hope that Valentine is proud of her mom. Prouder in any case than I've ever been of my mother. Every time I go back to see my parents, I feel like I'm slipping back down the social and material ladder I've been climbing so cautiously yet tenaciously. The minute I get to the station, I'm back in my childhood hand-me-downs: my voice trembles, my gestures are clumsy, and I feel annoyed. Profoundly annoyed, and it makes me wonder why, oh dear Lord, why do I inflict these visits on myself twice a month?

And with him, now, it's the same thing.

I'm back in my twenty-year-old skin. As if molting season were imminent, lurking in some corner of my native town or on the train, just waiting for me to lower my guard in order to attack. I remember Lucile, who used to work for me a few years ago. She was a tall, slim, attractive girl. One day she showed me photographs of her adolescent self. They used to call her Piglet or Butterball. She clenched her teeth while I looked at the shapeless mass of flesh in the photographs, and tried to discern the features of the woman she would become. She murmured that they were still inside her, Butterball and Piglet. She had to fight them off, every single day, all it took was a moment's inattention, if someone shoved past her in the Métro, or she took a little too long getting her credit card out of her wallet, and Butterball and Piglet would swoop down on her again. Chubby. Fat. Ugly. Useless.

As she was talking, I saw myself again, at the lycée and then afterward. I even think that that very evening, while talking to Lucile, I felt the shadow of Philippe Leduc brush over me. His insolence. His cruelty.

Philippe Leduc. Now there's someone who must have spent hours admiring himself in the mirror. Or maybe not. But in other people's eyes, yes. The supporting roles, only too happy to send his reflection back to him. But now. Look at you. The roles have been reversed. You shouldn't apologize for bumping into him. He is nothing to you. Nothing.

Today, he would be ready to eat out of your palm.

Today, he wouldn't dare treat you in an offhand manner.

I remember the party we went to together, of course— but I simply cannot recall the name of the boy who was throwing the party. Surely something like Arnaud or Christophe, those were the trendy names. His father was a doctor, that much I do remember. The mother worked with charities. They had money. Their house was on the edge of town. With a huge garden, and trees, and just beyond, fields stretching as far as the hills. It's all changed now. Houses have sprung up all around, the farms have been sold off, the town is spreading, bringing its supermarkets, its boulangeries that are not boulangeries, even warehouses that call themselves stores but which sell junk and knickknacks, everything for less than five euros. That house must be stuck in the middle of four other recent constructions, with the parents of the boy who invited us huddled inside. They'll end their lives trapped in a forest of shopping malls and parking lots.

I'm surprised at how spiteful I'm feeling.

I didn't think I'd be so bitter. There's no reason to be bitter nowadays. I have more money than the parents of Arnaud or Christophe will ever have—and I'm nowhere near the age of physical decline.

Maybe it was envy?

Yes.

After all, money meant self-confidence. So did good looks. I had neither. I was doing my best to become a shadow, a prompter at a theater—someone whose face you rarely see but who makes herself indispensable. I was thinking that sweetness and discretion would make me indispensable—to someone. To a boy. For a brief while I believed that boy might be Philippe Leduc. I clung to him, trying to keep myself light as air. And I went flying, with the first puff of wind.

The basement was turned into a disco, and between the rows of spotlights and the strobe, reality was garish and disjointed. For a while I watched people dancing, but the nearby loudspeakers were deafening, so I went upstairs. On the ground floor groups of students were lounging around and acting detached and cynical, as if they were rehearsing their roles as the next Jacques Dutronc or Bryan Ferry. Some of them had crowded around a table to play poker and drink liquor. Others were taking pictures of themselves, over and over, in the half-light of the living room. The French doors were open. I went outside for some air. Down at the end of the garden, you could hardly hear a thing. I liked walking in the grass. To feel it swishing against my shoes. A sweet feeling.

There were stars. It was easy to feel enchanted. I stared at a point on the horizon. He was standing in a corner over on my left, beneath the chestnut tree. I saw him only at the last minute. I was about to move away and, then I figured no, why should I. I had as much right to be there as he did. I murmured "Good evening." He smiled. We stood there for a while without speaking, but then suddenly that patch of garden felt crowded. We had to start talking, otherwise we'd seem ridiculous. I was looking for something to say. Something a bit less cheesy than, "I've always loved gardens in moonlight," or "When I was little, my father used to tell me the names of all the stars." Especially since it wasn't true. My father never gazed at stars either with me or on his own. And he didn't really contribute to my education. So I decided to be frank. And provocative, in a good-natured way.

"I thought you'd be in the basement all night."

"Don't judge a book by its cover."

"I hate proverbs and clichés."

"But sometimes they do reflect the truth."

"Sorry?"

"Well, look, if we're judging books by their covers, then you're the type of girl who spends all night out in the garden when there's a party going on in the house."

I could have been annoyed or even shocked, but instead I thought it was a clever answer. I laughed. And added, "Score one for Philippe Leduc." And I sensed him relaxing ever so faintly. His shoulders dropping slightly.

"And a point for you, too, for knowing my name."

"Everyone who was at the lycée with you knows your name."

"Only half a point then."

"And two points for you if you know my name."

"First and last?"

"One point for first, one point for last."

"Or maybe one and a half points for first, and—"

"Stop trying to buy time. You may as well give up right away."

I was facing him. I was smiling. It wasn't hard to smile at him. Just staring at him made you feel like seducing him. I must have had little bubbles in my eyes, something sparkling. The situation was entertaining. He'd been caught in his own trap. And I'd managed to catch him off guard. Suddenly I could see why he might be interested: here was a girl who knew how to answer back, who was sharp. Sometimes that can even make up for average looks. Especially at night. I knew that two or three days from now he would feel embarrassed. And ashamed, so he'd go and blame the alcohol and the late hour. But for the moment, I had a goal. I wondered if I'd manage to reach it. It was exciting.

I thought of the Leap of Death. At my grandmother's, when I was little: the Leap of Death used to take my breath away. It was a challenge I'd made up, a game that consisted in jumping down several steps of the stone stairway without falling, to land on the path in the garden. You started with just one step, then two, three, four. The Leap of Death was five whole steps. Every time, I imagined my face would be covered in blood, the grown-ups would come rushing out, my mother would scream with despair, my father would practically pass out, my schoolmates (who, inexplicably, had suddenly shown up, too) would be crying their young eyes out. Ecstasy. The ecstasy of the instant before the Leap of Death, because now I would have to go through with it, after all.

So I moved a few inches closer and held out my hand.

"Pleased to meet you. My name is Cécile Duffaut. Repeat after me, Cé-cile Duf-faut."

"Hey, I hadn't given up yet, as far as I know."

"Too late."

He took my hand. He held it in his. It was an awkward moment, but when you're post-adolescent, you enjoy these awkward moments. You feel as if things can change dramatically. And they often do.

"I am delighted to make your acquaintance, Cé-cile Duf-faut."

"I'm not."

"Sorry?"

"I'm delighted, but I'm not making your acquaintance."

So bold, all of a sudden.

I have this boldness in me. Deep-rooted. I stifled it for years, smothered it to keep it buried, but it comes out with the explosiveness of a champagne cork whenever I feel a certain pressure, the way I did then. Now I know how to use it to my advantage. It's very useful in meetings, negotiations, sales contracts. Sometimes it makes my colleagues or competitors blush, but basically they like to see a display of nerve. A sharpness of tone. The sharp edge of the guillotine.

Philippe Leduc began to laugh heartily.

Men always think that once they've made a woman laugh, they're already halfway to her bed—and they don't realize how much the opposite holds true as well.

Was Philippe Leduc worth it?

At the age of twenty, perhaps he was.

It's a difficult age, twenty, for a man. They're so eager to dominate. To mark their territory. There's a sort of nervous abruptness. Awkwardness. That rebellious side, inspiring tenderness but unbearable at the same time.

It's a difficult age, but that's no excuse.

In any case, it's no excuse for London.

I'm feeling a sudden surge of rage.

So I really haven't gotten over it.

On the 6:41 train, in the toilet, looking in the mirror, I remember the journey home.

By the time I walked out of the station, all alone, I was seething. Sitting in the sidewalk café across the street was Mathieu. Philippe Leduc's best friend. A mere coincidence. We had met a few times. Now we exchanged hesitant greetings. He frowned. He asked me where I had been. London. With Philippe? I waved my hand as if to say, "It's not important." He asked me if I wanted a coffee. I almost said no, because it wasn't a good time, I had other fish to fry, I had some wild horses inside me that wanted setting free, but I shrugged and said "Why not?" I toyed with the idea of seducing Mathieu. It gave me pleasure. I didn't go any further, because I wasn't that sort of girl. Nowadays I wouldn't hesitate.

Mathieu.

Mathieu Coché.

I would never even have remembered his name if I hadn't come across an article in a magazine at the hairdresser's. A fairly long interview. A rising star, describing his childhood. His adolescence. His roots. His passion for the theater. How he moved to Paris, and all the opportunities there. It was mush. Sickly sweet. A cream pie of the sort you like to lap up while you're waiting for the hairdresser to finish painting your hair with dye.

I looked at the photograph, and I didn't recognize

the young man I had known. Back in those days Mathieu Coché was not particularly popular or even attractive. He seemed gauche. A bit of a lump is how my grandmother would have put it. Burdened with a frame that was shooting up, but that, for the time being, was too well-filled. He often looked downcast. He had an identity only by virtue of association. He was "Philippe Leduc's friend". He was just a stand-in, and girls showed any interest in him only because of his closeness to the boy they really coveted.

What a magnificent role reversal.

I didn't really follow Mathieu's career; I kept up with the programs on television, but I don't think I ever saw a single film or series he played in. The insipid nature of the article annoyed me. I was just about to put the magazine down when I noticed the mole he had just above his wrist. I don't know why, but it affected me. I smiled. I smiled at the man in the photograph. That day, too, at the hairdresser's, I remembered the sidewalk café opposite the train station.

We didn't really know what to talk about. Mathieu Coché wasn't very chatty. I was really surprised, too, when I found out he'd become an actor. The way I saw it, actors had to be extroverts, had to feel easy around people. Performers who were well-integrated and experienced in giving interviews.

I was seething with hatred that day. With no end in sight. It had overwhelmed me on the return journey. I had emerged from the sort of hazy state I'd been in most of the night. I was only vaguely aware of getting off the train in Dover, showing my passport, and boarding another train. But suddenly in Paris, when I left the Gare du Nord, there was a wolfhound in my body. If Leduc had been there in front of me, I would have torn him to shreds.

I felt just the same—nothing had changed—when I got off the train in Troyes. Then suddenly there was Mathieu Coché. The guy's best friend. It was too much. But at the same time I knew I had no reason to blame Mathieu. Besides, he was being considerate. He asked me, awkwardly, had it not gone well. I just said, "You don't want to know," and he nodded. He let a few minutes go by. The waiters were bustling around us. With their black and gold striped waistcoats, they looked like wasps.

I saw wasps. All around me. Their mandibles slicing up pieces of my flesh with a precise cruelty. My arms. My cheeks. My tongue. My eyes.

I had a sudden abrupt reaction, and almost knocked over the table. Mathieu Coché was startled. He touched my hand.

"What's wrong?"

"Nothing. I thought there was an insect."

"If you want to talk, or have a drink, or simply see someone, you can call me. I'll be here all summer."

I didn't say anything. I just stared at him. What was he thinking, really? Was he trying to hit on me? Was this his thing, to console the ex-girlfriends of his pal the heartbreaker? Or was it nothing? Simply nothing? Politeness? Kindness in the presence of someone who's in pain? I never found out. I never called him, either.

He raised his hand to ask for the check, and the watch he was wearing slipped an inch or so down his arm. That's when I saw the mole, just above his wrist.

All of a sudden, I emerged from my hatred.

I caught a glimpse of what was hidden deep inside Mathieu Coché.

His eyes, shoulders, forearms, neck—everything was seeping with absence. With emptiness.

The possibility, suddenly, of another life, with Mathieu Coché, was dizzying. Even today, it still is. Even here, now, on this early-morning train. Even here in these SNCF toilets that could use a good cleaning.

Someone just tried the handle. Once. Twice.

I don't know how long I've been in here.

I'm out of my mind.

I have to get out of here. And back to my seat. The trip is already half over. It will go quickly now. Everything goes so fast anyway. Everything goes so fast, but twenty-seven years later, it is all still there.

"Excuse me."
"No problem."

She brushed past me.

Just the slightest contact, that brushing motion, bringing back impressions, colors, dark green, deep blue, undergrowth. Did I ever go walking in the forest with Cécile? If I did, I don't remember. And yet there's a lot I do remember. Some things that I would rather forget. The way I behaved toward her at the end. I would like to tell her that I never did anything like that ever again. It's true. Before her, yes. I could be a real lout. A cad. All those words no one uses much anymore.

I was almost back there.

If I closed my eyes, with her legs brushing against mine, I could remember how it was, the two of us. The way we moved together. The way we talked. All that blustering. How we wanted to make fun of everything. To be supremely ironic. Such vanity. What poseurs we were.

My cell phone vibrating.

Text message from Christine: "We have to talk." Which just goes to show how useful cell phones are: to send a message to tell the other person that you have to talk. Now, indeed, the time has come to be sarcastic. But sarcasm all on one's own is pointless. And this woman next to me on the train is not about to speak to me. I wonder if she's recognized me. I'll bet she has, now: but that's pure vanity. As if I were so unforgettable. And my looks hadn't changed a bit. That's what I used to think. That as you got older your body just got drier—you got wrinkles, more accentuated features, and that was it. Whereas nowadays I look like a balloon. Full of hot air, wedged tight into an uncomfortable SNCF seat.

What am I supposed to say to Christine? What can I possibly reply? "Whenever you want," "Yes," "No," "Now what," "I miss you."

Or something neutral and descriptive. "I'm on the train." Then, for a bit of spice, provoke her: "With Cécile Duffaut." But that wouldn't serve any purpose—Christine doesn't know Cécile.

And besides, this encounter is purely anecdotal. There are other women I could have run into on the train. Women who have actually meant something in my life. Virginie, for example. Who I was seeing before Christine. We were together for two years. We had a lot in common. And a lot of differences—it would have been impossible to construct anything on such a swamp, and already back then I wanted something solid, concrete, a protection against erosion. Or Élise. That's true, there was Élise. Only one month, but a month of breathtaking intensity. She was about to go to Brazil, she had a round-trip ticket good for a year, but she wasn't at all sure she would come back, she'd been dreaming about Brazil since she was a kid. One night she said to me, "You could go, too, you could drop everything and come with me." She smiled as she said it. She knew it was just idle talk. I'm not the type who can do that sort of thing. In fact, I don't know anyone in my circle who could just go off like that. On a wild impulse: you only see that sort of thing in fiction, in bad novels, Sunday evening TV movies. I wonder where Élise is now. I can't picture her old. There's a good chance she's not even old. She could be dead, for all I know. Long dead. That's what I'm afraid of. You meet someone, you're together for a while, then he or she disappears from your everyday life, you get over it, you forget. One day, on a train, you think, "For all I know, they're dead." I'm glad to be traveling here silently with Cécile Duffaut: at least I know she's not dead.

In spite of everything, I'm also glad I'm on my way to see Mathieu. Because the two of us know exactly where we stand. And I'll never have to say, "Well, for all I know he's dead." At least that.

At least that.

I hate that expression more than anything. My mother uses it all the time. It reassures her about the world around her. Gives it logic, seemliness. But she can take it way too far. When the space shuttle Challenger exploded, out it came: at least their bodies won't be endlessly orbiting the earth. And once she managed to tear her eyes away from the screen after the planes had crashed into the twin towers, she murmured, at least they had time to call their wives and husbands to say good-bye.

I'm an At Least son.

At least you passed your exams.

At least you've got a steady job.

At least you've had children.

At least your ex-wife isn't making a fuss about the alimony.

At least your divorce hasn't gone too badly.
At least you're not dead.

I did almost die, once.
Like everyone, I suppose.
I was sailing on the lake, ten miles or so from my parents' place. It was not long after Cécile Duffaut. A sudden storm. The wind picked up, formed a tornado. I was fascinated. I'd never seen one in my life. After that I don't know exactly what happened. Something bashed me in the back of the head, probably the boom jibing. I passed out and fell overboard. The other sailors didn't have time to notice me: their boats were in trouble, too. I opened my eyes: algae, bubbles, silt, but the terrifying noise of the storm was gone. It felt good, there. I felt good. I thought, game over, and I think I smiled, but is it possible to smile when you're running out of air? I remember that my head hurt, and I may well have been bleeding.

I didn't want to die, but living wasn't all that great an option, either. My relationships with girls were heading nowhere. My parents and I annoyed each other beyond belief. The years seemed to be frittering away, like the friendships I had thought would always endure. Anything could happen, why not death?

But I rose to the surface. A moment of panic. Air. The need for air. But it was a close call. I've never been out sailing since.

Of course everything would be different now. I have responsibilities. I have my children.

I can still hear that white noise distinctly—not

unlike the crackling of a vinyl record once the music is over. The silence of afterward. Almost religious. And mocking, too.

I have my children.

The verb "to have." It's a troublesome one. It's not a verb I'm familiar with. The more time goes by, the more I lose. The more I lose, the freer I am. The freer I am the more I wish I weren't so free. What am I supposed to do with all this freedom?

Make Cécile an offer, for example.

I'll turn to face her and I'll explain myself. I'll tell her about Mathieu. About me, my children, Christine, about how life takes sudden strange turns.

I'll apologize for London.

Because of course I remember.

We'll go back over all that, get things off our chests, I'll manage to cheer her up, she'll forget that she's a busy married woman, a mother, I'll throw down the gauntlet, Cécile, let's go back to London, right now, I'll make you forget that trip we took together, have you ever been back to London, Cécile? It's a great city, you know. No, don't tell me I ruined it for you. I did? No! Really? Then we have to fix that, whaddya say, right away, let's drop everything—work, spouse, kids—and disappear for forty-eight hours to England, or more, if we get along.

Are you up for it?

You're on.

Right now.

Well, two or three minutes from now.

However long it takes for me to get used to the idea
of such a sudden departure, together.

No, I had something to do with it, too.

I shouldn't be disingenuous. I wasn't the type of girl who had men turning around as I walked by. And I didn't do anything to encourage them. I preferred wearing baggy clothes and shapeless sweatshirts; guys must've thought I spent my weekends sprawled in front of the television. And so they were often pleasantly surprised when I took my clothes off. And discovered that I actually had a figure.

Plus shyness.

No, that's not it, either. I've never thought of myself as shy. It was just I didn't feel like struggling for hours to impose my taste or my point of view, to defend a particular film or rock band or politician. It all seemed useless. I would look at them, all those strutting peacocks, puffing out their chests and crowing louder than anyone. And sometimes there in the barnyard a few hens would cackle as they pecked around the cocks, and the peahens would spread their feathers, because their song was so horrible; and then there were the graylag geese. *Pasionarias* who took every subject to heart, and they could easily go up an octave to stand up to the kings of the farm, another way of getting attention, of displaying their charms. And it worked. Men like it when you stand up to them. It arouses their hunting instinct. I wasn't that kind.

I was worse.

I was one of those girls who are said to have a blank gaze, simply because behind our expressionless masks we hide our true contempt for all the jousting, for all those tinsel princesses and papier-mâché knights in shining armor. And for ourselves, above all. My self-contempt was equal to my disdain for them. A pretty picture.

But it didn't show, at all.

I know what people said about me in those days. She's nice. She's easygoing. Not the sharpest knife in the drawer. Quiet. Reserved. A little empty, maybe. Having said that, you can always count on her.

And in bed, did any of that cross his mind, Philippe Leduc? No. He would only have been thinking about his erection, which he had trouble maintaining. He must have been conjuring images of girls who were flashier than me—famous actresses, rocker chicks in leather pants—and his only aim would have been to stay hard, as long as possible. And to what end? Not for my pleasure, surely, he couldn't have cared less. Not even for his own. Just out of pride. So he could say, "Sure, I scored."

Don't you think we might have missed something then, Philippe?

Because our bodies were a good fit; because there were times you managed to forget your fear, your obsession with performance, because our skin would touch and the tenderness that came from that caress surprised both of us. We didn't know that life is long, that our alliances would change, and that, anyway, over time we'd lose that urge to boast. We didn't know we might have been a good match, one of those couples who understand each other intimately, who exchange knowing glances when other people go on and on.

Do you at least remember what it was like afterward?

After lovemaking. My hand on your chest. The sweat on your shoulder. My fingers going down then up again. Neck, belly, cock, still damp. Your chest rising and falling. And your eyes. The thankfulness as you looked at me. Really looked, deep inside me.

And everything was so easy afterward. Conversation flowed. Moving naked around the room—it all seemed natural. I liked your body. That's why I remember it so well. Before you came along there were other bodies that left me indifferent, but others still that almost made me want to laugh. None that caught my imagination. And afterward, it was the same old story. I admired Luc's body, of course—he seemed to be made for sex. But never again would I find that sense of the familiar that I had with your body.

I'm talking to you, Philippe. This is a declaration, from twenty-seven years away, this is a declaration even though you don't look at all the way you used to, even though no one notices you anymore, and you've sunken into the anonymity of your fifties where we seem to go all gray and hazy—hardly anyone notices, except for the occasional cruel comment: "He must have been a handsome man," "I'll bet she was stunning."

I'm talking to you and you can't hear me.

I'm trying to be ironic.

I'm trying to stop this little wave that is building inside and which is threatening to swell and turn into a breaker just as we reach the port—the Gare de l'Est, thirty minutes from now, I've just glanced at my watch. Thirty minutes left to dive in, into the flotsam of the years gone by, and hope to find a piece of wood, a roof, a boat adrift—to start everything all over again.

What on earth am I saying?

Anything but that.

Remember the last night in London. Remember the tone of his voice in the room that night. And all the preceding afternoon. How impatient he was. You weren't interesting anymore. He wasn't attracted to you anymore. Words hurled like javelins. Hurtful comments, about the way you dressed, your lack of polish, of shine, "an ant in a patch of grass, not even the Queen ant, oh no, anything but, just one ant among all the other ants, the ant par excellence, no critical distance, no ambition, nothing to make you stand out among the others."

I remember every word.

Which doesn't surprise me.

I had buried them in my memory. I'd struggled against them, but I knew very well that I hadn't destroyed them.

Where did it come from, all that scorn? Couldn't you simply have come out with a few harmless statements, just acted embarrassed, and told me it was over? Remained dignified? I would have rolled with the punches. Sure, I'd become attached, after four months—but I was still realistic. I had always known that sooner or later you would get tired of me.

You wanted to go back to Camden Town. We had been there the night before; I thought it was kind of seedy and not all that interesting. I sighed. I would have preferred to wander around Chelsea or Belgravia. Wander aimlessly, to see how the locals lived, to allow myself to melt—you were right, and that's what hurt the most—allow myself to melt into the background. I sighed, and you exploded. The famous last straw. Or the straw that broke the camel's back. Or the ant, forever lost in the haystack.

The ant.

Did you know I still think about that, a lot?

You never imagine that certain phrases can stick, buried in your skin like splinters, and that at certain moments in life they come back and wreck everything.

My grandfather had fought at Verdun. He was very young. A shell exploded a few yards away from him. He had shrapnel in his legs all his life, and from time to time, with the changing seasons, a shell fragment would say, *Give him my kind regards.*

Those two words were my shell fragments.

Some years ago, maybe eight or nine, Valentine was in primary school, we came home one evening and the kitchen had been invaded by thousands of flying ants. They had built a nest under the sink in a hole in the wall and we hadn't noticed. Valentine was screaming and there I was, the one who was usually solid as a rock in our family, the one who knew how to lay tiles, mix plaster, change a tire better than Luc, or talk about horsepower and aerodynamics, there I was, the woman who could tell off telemarketers and nosey real estate agents: I went to pieces. Because of some flying ants, treating me like their equal, crawling all over me, welcoming me in their midst, at last you're back. For a few minutes I lost my mind.

Valentine remembers.

Luc, too.

If he hadn't come home just in time, I don't know what would have happened.

And yet I fought it.

I did nothing else, after I got back from London. Everything was very clear in my mind. The things I would no longer put up with. Who I would become. Every decision I made that night I followed to the letter. Those decisions gave structure to my life. Gave meaning to the direction I was headed in. Never again would I be an ant. Never again would I taste that bitterness.

No one, today, would dare to compare me to an ant. Not a single person I know would ever think of such a thing.

The only one who sometimes still feels the shell, the formic acid, the little legs wriggling: that's me, and me alone—and it's because of you, Philippe Leduc.

I ought to tell you.

I shift slightly toward you in my seat.

You look so lost. You haven't even noticed that I'm looking at you. You're in one of those moments when everything goes slack—muscles, skin, consciousness; your mind wanders and disappointment accumulates, along with feelings of failure. There is only one thing a person feels like doing when they see you like that, you know, and that would be to put their arm around your shoulder and tell you not to worry, everything will turn out all right.

And you must be thinking about the person you never became, that sharp, brilliant man you seemed destined to become. Someone who would leave their mark. Who would pose for magazines. Like Mathieu Coché. Is that what you're thinking, Philippe? About how you've failed—and with a vengeance—and you've ended up on the 6:41 train, like me?

Except that thanks to you I am not what I seem. Even if the ant inside me did drive me to travel second class, yet again, when really I could easily have afforded first.

With your face only a few inches from mine, I'm trying to sound you out, but I can't.

You're unfathomable, Leduc.

That's the least of your faults.

We would take the Eurostar.

The Eurostar, which didn't exist back then, when the two of us went to London.

I had no regrets.

That's the worst of it, I think. Now I do, of course, but at the time, I didn't. I thought good riddance, or something like that. Classy. I was very classy, in those days. I was very sure of everything.

She had begun to annoy me, probably even before we left for London. Little things. The way she would stare at the floor while I was talking to her. The fact that she preferred films where nothing happened. This derisive side she had—she would look at me out of the corner of her eye, and I could tell she didn't believe in flirtation for a minute. Her discreet irony. I needed to be admired. To be set on a pedestal.

I'm not looking for excuses.

And then, she was gaining power.

Insidiously.

She was nothing to look at, with her ordinary face, slightly curly shoulder length hair, and clothes that came straight from a discount superstore. She would listen to me talking. People who listen always end up in a position of superiority; they don't share their secrets, they remain whole, intact, whereas you've allowed your flaws to show through.

And then she—

No, it's really hard to remember this.

Years later, it's still hard to come out and admit it.

It's crazy how sex can still haunt you even after so much time has gone by.

How should I put it? She knew how to relax me? Make me hard? Make me stay hard? Reassure me? All of that at the same time. I should have been grateful. But it was the opposite. I felt sure that some day she would go and make fun of me, in public. Which was idiotic. But when you're twenty years old, you have no critical distance, your vision is really limited to what's close-up, there before you.

I was so relieved when she slammed the door that night.

There I was in the London night. Alone and accompanied at the same time. I had a headache. The alcohol made my gestures uncertain—and yet, I was relieved.

One less burden.

And now I don't understand. I don't understand myself.

I'll talk about it with Mathieu.

It'll be a good topic of conversation, for a start. Maybe by going back over all this old stuff, by bringing the world of a quarter of a century ago back to life, we'll manage to get through thirty or forty minutes. An hour. And after that, he'll be calm. Yes, that's a good idea, I'll talk to him about Cécile Duffaut.

I'm afraid.

I know I am because the vein on the right-hand side of my neck has started throbbing.

Unless it's a nerve.

Do we have nerves in our neck?

I don't know what sort of state I'll find him in.

My last visit was ten days ago. He wants me to come more often. He wants me to be there every day. He would like everyone to be there every day, but now that he's in the hospital, the others don't come anymore. Sometimes they call. They send presents. They send text messages. But they don't actually go. Something always comes up. They were all ready to go, it was all planned, cross my heart and hope to die, we'll be there tomorrow afternoon, and two hours before they were supposed to be there, with Mathieu getting more and more impatient, they call and say they're really sorry, their voices full of contrition, but really, they simply can't make it, a really important program, an appointment that could change their life, the dishwasher has broken down completely unexpectedly and the kitchen is flooded. Mathieu smiles valiantly (and I feel like shouting: "Mathieu, you're on the *phone*, they can't see you, stop smiling"), then says again in a weary little voice that it doesn't matter, it's no big deal, some other time, and he finds excuses for them after all, it's true, they have to get on with their lives.

I don't say anything.

I think: with me it's different.

I'm trying to sound ironic, with limited success. Because it's true, after all, with me it's different.

I don't have anything special to do, other than my job and my divorced family.

Mathieu's cancer is an event.

I have such a thrilling life.

It started a few months ago now. Not long after he broke up with Astrid. He wasn't in great shape. He was losing weight, which was normal, he was hardly eating. He didn't feel like going out, or having people over. He had headaches all the time. Even he was surprised. He didn't think their breakup would affect him so much.

"How long did it last in all?"

"Ten months. A year."

"On the scale of a lifetime ..."

"I know. That's why I don't understand why I can't get my act together."

"You're getting old."

"I suppose. And besides, you know, when I think of you with your kids, I tell myself that maybe I've missed out on something."

"Well, me and my kids, it's not as if we're together all that much. They've found a dad who is exactly what they were looking for."

"Don't say that. You know very well that everyone only has one dad."

"I'm not so sure."

"Well, I'll never know, since I'm not a father."

"How do you know? You've left your sperm in a fair share of women."

"I'm being serious."

"Just look at the life you lead. What would you do with a kid? Kids need stability, guidance, routine."

"Depends on the kid."

I broke off the discussion. I could tell it wasn't going anywhere. To change tack, I said, "Maybe you should see a doctor. You never know, it might have nothing to do with Astrid. It might only be physical."

Mathieu liked the idea that it might "only be physical." Some other thing that wouldn't weigh on his mind. Rational. Explainable. Medical.

He liked it a lot less when the results came in.

He'd lain in bed for hours. He called me. He had a strange metallic voice. Like the Tin Man in the *Wizard of Oz*. I took the first train, the same 6:41. It was in the middle of the February school break. I moved into his place. We talked the way we'd never talked before. Whenever I went out to go shopping or just to have a break, he would try to call people he knew, people I'd met at parties. The ones he got hold of were full of sympathy. His life seemed sad to me.

I sat in cafés in Paris and wrote letters to my children. Some day I may send them. But what would they make of them? In the letters I referred to a whole list of unfamiliar names, people they've never met, places they've never seen. When parents tell their stories it's anything but clear, and it's probably better that way. I toyed with the idea of writing a novel, too. I don't have the talent. Nor, in all likelihood, the desire.

I wonder how Cécile gets along with her children. I see my kids only in brief spurts now that they've moved. No, that's not fair. I don't think it's really because of the change, or because of their new stepfather. It's their age. They're learning to keep their distance. One day Loïc and I went to visit the cathedral. He was three or four years old. He couldn't have cared less about the building. All he could see was the yellow balloon I had just bought for him. One of those helium balloons with a white plastic wand. I like hanging around the cathedral. That's where I kissed my first conquest, behind a pillar. I've always thought there was something erotic about churches: the silence, the cool air, the stone, the fact that someone might go by, the feverishness, the transgression. I was thinking back about that moment. I was wondering what had become of that girl I kissed, whom I never saw again—or if I did, I didn't recognize her. Loïc let go of his balloon, right there in the nave. Up, up, up went the balloon, all the way to the rose window, and then higher still, until it got stuck beneath a gothic arch, way above our heads. It looked tiny. There was no way we could reach it. Loïc was inconsolable. He didn't want another one to replace it. He went home, crestfallen.

The next day I went back to the cathedral. The balloon was still there, hardly visible. I went back every day. I don't know why. I figured that sooner or later it would burst or deflate and end up back on the ground—and then, I would take the plastic remains to my son. He would smile and keep them. One evening, the balloon was gone. Not a trace, either on the ground or in the air.

Children are like that. Like helium balloons in

cathedrals. Let go of them, and they will fly off, but they're still in sight, you wave to them, you visit them, and they're way up there, far away, still stuck beneath our gothic arches. Then one day, and you never quite know why, they're no longer anywhere to be seen.

No.

Stop feeling sorry for yourself.

You're not going to start blubbering, on the 6:41 train next to Cécile Duffaut.

Although.

It could get a conversation going.

No.

There are simpler ways.

Drop something.

A book, a tissue, a pencil: she would pick it up, we would look at each other, recognize each other, life flowing into our bodies, and our paths change direction.

"Excuse me, I ... I ... I mean, my pen—"

"Go right ahead."

"Ah, there it is ... I've got it ... you ... excuse me, but isn't your name Cécile Duffaut?"

"Mergey."

"Sorry?"

"Mergey. That's my married name. Cécile Mergey."

"Ah, yes, of course, I see. Sorry. I am—"

"I know who you are."

"Ah. Good. That's good, yes, good."

"Is it?"

I know.

I didn't think I'd react like that.

That I'd be so sharp, and interrupt the conversation before it even got started.

And turn my head so ostensibly to the window—no point dwelling on it now.

I am not kind.

But all the images suddenly rose to the surface.

Everything I had buried for years. The way the events unfolded.

We were in the cafeteria at the modern art museum—the Tate Gallery, that was it, the names are coming back. It was a strange room with mirrors on the walls, so our reflections were multiplied ad infinitum. I was suffocating. We hadn't said a word to each other for several minutes. We could sense the end was drawing near; I still couldn't understand when it was that everything had suddenly changed, but it no longer mattered. Our four-month adventure would be ending there, and it was a pity, we could have made a fine couple, but anyway, I was aware of his change of attitude, the hurtful words, and I was withdrawing, accepting the fact it was over. I finished my tea—I had ordered tea even though I hate tea, simply because I was there, in London, and the moment itself was hateful—the smell of it made me feel sick—everything did, suddenly, that city, that country, that language, the man next to me staring absently into the reflections in the mirror. I said, "I'm going back to the hotel," and there was no answer. I wasn't expecting one.

My initial thought was that I would pack my bags and take the next train back to France. But when I realized that it would mean spending the night sitting up in an uncomfortable railway car, to be woken at one o'clock in the morning to take the cross-Channel ferry, then disembark at three o'clock in the morning, French time, to take the train from Calais to Paris, change stations in the fog then take another train for Troyes, and reach my destination late in the morning—broken, wounded, in pain,—no, I couldn't do it. And anyway, I was sure that Philippe would not come back to the hotel. And if he did come back, then it would be to get things out in the open. Or to apologize. Maybe he would want me to reassure him again. He would want me to wait, with my lips against his shoulder. He would want us to be close again. Because, like an idiot, I still had this tiny hope. Not much. But still. I was sure we were missing out on a meaningful relationship. A real adventure. And that it hadn't even begun yet.

The bed-and-breakfast was in a quiet neighborhood. Bloomsbury. Cartwright Gardens. I can still remember the name of the street. It wasn't actually a street, but a crescent of buildings looking onto a tiny park with a completely incongruous tennis court, there in the center of London.

We had found it completely by chance, leafing

through a guidebook in a bookstore in France. It was more than we could afford, but we decided we'd do without any souvenirs or presents for our friends in Troyes. A fortunate intuition.

I would have thrown everything out.

And yet.

During the night, I went to an all-night corner store and bought some water, a packet of cookies, a few snacks and, almost as an afterthought, a key ring. Two flags, the Union Jack and the English flag, the St. George's Cross. I kept it for a long time. I wish I could say I had it on me at this very moment now that I'm reminiscing about all that. It would be so romantic—when in fact it was anything but. But I can't. Valentine commandeered it when she was in high school, for the key to her locker, and she lost it. At the time, I didn't even think about it. I just argued with her because she'd lost the lock.

And now I miss it. How stupid is that.

So we went to stay at this bed-and-breakfast that was too expensive. The room was old-fashioned and rundown; the sash windows didn't close properly, the wall-to-wall carpet was patched here and there, and the wallpaper had seen better days—but there was a tiny balcony that looked out on the rooftops. That's where I sat when I came back alone. I watched the evening descend in the English sky: clouds, swaths of clear sky, a warm wind, purple, blue, pink, yellow. I repeated the proverb I had learned a few years earlier, *Every cloud has a silver lining*. I tried to find the French equivalent:

À quelque chose, Malheur est bon; Après la pluie, le beau temps. Misfortune is good for something; after the rain, fine weather.

I wanted some fine weather.

I sat right on the concrete balcony, my knees bent, my arms around my legs, and I hardly took up any room. I listened to the sounds of the city, the hubbub, and from time to time the dissonant note of an ambulance or the siren of a fire truck. Down in the park in Cartwright Gardens, a couple was diligently playing tennis. She played better than he did. Sometimes she would have him repeat his moves, drive, backhand. Before long they had to stop, it was getting dark.

I could feel a tingling in my fingertips.

I didn't want to be an observer anymore. Someone who absorbs. Someone who keeps to one side and stares out at the spectacle of the world with indifference. I wanted to be in the world. Really in it. I didn't want to be an artist. I wanted to be a protagonist. I wanted to live passionately, with love and hate and scorn, I wanted to throw myself on the bed weeping floods of tears, tearing my hair out in despair, jumping for joy, flinging my arms around people, holding their hands, holding a hand—and leading the dance.

Contrary to all expectations, it was a tender moment. One of those rare moments when you take the time to think about what is all right, and what isn't all right, and what could change, and what should change: you see the paths forming, and how to make your way past the swampy terrain.

The breakup was definite but I went to bed feeling calmer; I had packed my bag and was ready to go. The next morning I would leave a note on the night table or, if by chance Philippe had come back, I would place my hand on his forehead and say, "No hard feelings. See you around." Unless. Then we'd have to see. Lay down conditions. Nothing like this, ever again.

I fell asleep in that state of mind.

The window was open, and I was in harmony with the city. Noise, fatigue, but also a tremendous desire for change. A desire to become someone else. Someone good. Or at least respected. The process had begun. It should have gone on naturally, taken its course in the months and years to come. In fact, the birth went very quickly.

And the obstetrician ruined everything.

I can feel my lips tightening with the first signs of the outskirts of Paris.

This is where I live now, the outskirts of Paris, along with hundreds of thousands of other people. But I am not an ant. I know what I want. And above all I know what I don't want.

You, Philippe.
I don't want anything to do with you.

Memories overlapping.

What an exhausting trip.

I didn't need this.

The one thing I dream of, when we get to Paris, would be to find a hotel and sleep in an anonymous, comfortable room, where nobody would want anything from me. I would take the exit behind the Gare de l'Est, the one no one uses—Château-Landon—and book the first available room at the All Seasons, the elevator would be full of Japanese tourists out for a good time, and I would collapse on the bed. And when I woke up I'd be another person.

I really would like to be another person.

I've always wanted to be another person. Less disciplined. More intelligent. Brilliant. A meteor. Someone you see whiz by in the sky and you talk about them to your kids years later, all starry-eyed. Someone like Mathieu Coché. And yet it's strange, when we were teenagers, you would never have expected anything like it. Mathieu was sort of my sparring partner. The guy who comes along with you to auditions to read you your lines, but who never gets chosen. I don't know what made the difference. Adversity, perhaps. Nothing was easy for him back then, whereas for me, everything just landed in my lap—love, friendship, sex, it was all dead simple. Cécile Duffaut was actually the first girl who ever left me. How could she have done anything else?

I was unbearable.

I remember the end, in London. Don't think I don't. You might think you've forgotten everything, but that would be blatant hypocrisy. In fact, I'm convinced that people's ability to remember is much better than they claim.

I wandered around, it was late afternoon. At first I was glad to be alone. At that age it's hard to explain to the person you're with that you might need solitude, that you don't want to be glued to them twenty-four hours a day. This was the first time we'd been together for whole days at a time. In a foreign city. I suppose it could have brought us closer if we had really been in love. But that wasn't the case. I say, "I suppose," because the more time goes by, the more I wonder if I've ever been in love. It was as if I was wrapped in a thin layer of plastic that kept me apart from other people. But maybe it's the same for everyone. Every human being must wonder what it means "to be in love." What came closest, for me, was a desire to spend my everyday life with another person: morning breath, the coziness of a night without sex, breakfast for two and then for four, X-Factor programs on TV on Saturday evenings. I know there's nothing at all exciting about any of that.

In fact, I could easily have shared my everyday life with Cécile Duffaut. We got along well. It's just that when you're twenty that's not enough. You dream about things that'll blow you sky-high, full of incredible passion, you want to be beside yourself with emotion and euphoria and pain, your heart beating wildly.

You're convinced that unless you're experiencing all that you must be heading down the wrong path, and the relationship is not worth the effort.

And then after a while you realize it's not going to happen.

So either you become resigned, or you make believe. You waltz around like some nineteenth century heroine, sighing, moaning, weeping—and you lie. And all around you, people call it love.

With Christine there was never any of that. No love at first sight. We hung out with the same group of friends. So we saw a lot of each other and eyed each other and circled around each other for months. I invited her to a party. We went home together. Everything flowed, it was all completely natural. Since then I've been thinking of love as something that flows.

Did it flow between Cécile and me?

Yes.

There's a woman in her thirties a bit farther down the car; she looks tired. A child asleep with its head on her lap.

Yes.

An adolescent nodding his head, listening to some music the other passengers will never hear, but in his ears it's exploding.

Yes.

An older man muttering to himself while he reads a magazine about the private lives of the rich and famous.

Yes.

And the two of us, sitting next to each other—we could have been a couple. We could have made believe.

But I'm not sure that Cécile Duffaut is the sort of woman who would make believe. She's recognized me. She doesn't want to speak to me. She's right.

I was almost at the hotel. I could see her on the balcony. I didn't feel like going in, explaining, negotiating, arguing. I thought she would have packed her bags. I went to a pub on the corner of the street. I don't remember the name, just the color. Red, with gilded letters.

It was starting to fill up with locals. I drank three or four pints. Enough to tear down the language barrier. I fraternized with a group of Brits my age who were planning a trip to France to go girl-hunting, because it was a well-known fact, aah, those French girls, etc.

Jerks.

The kind you find in every country.

You find them mainly in bars, after office hours. Herds of guys, with their coarse laughter, spilling booze on their T-shirts, and saying they'll do anything to get laid. I couldn't understand half of what these guys were saying but it hardly mattered. I felt good. I was a jerk. I'm not saying this out of bitterness. Or out of scorn. It's just a fact.

One of them was making racist jokes about Pakistanis, and I laughed like an idiot. Laughed, maybe, but I was uncomfortable all the same, because back in France I wouldn't have put up with intolerance. Later that evening I spoke with this guy Andrew, who was quieter. He was getting drunk methodically, to forget that he hadn't had a girlfriend in over a year. The two of us went on to a nightclub.

It was one of those unlikely sorts of discotheques that you sometimes come across in Anglo-Saxon countries. A church turned into a dance floor. A place of worship, for the body, for appearance. The atmosphere was distinctly different, depending on whether you were in the chapel or the nave. In the nave, the music took up all the space and the light was dazzling; it was crowded and it was hard to make your way to the bar. The bass was pounding in your ears and you couldn't think straight. Andrew didn't want to dance. He sat down on one of the wooden pews the designer had preserved. He guzzled beer after beer, staring into space. At one point, he vanished. I can still see his face, just as he was. I picture him married and divorced with one kid, the manager of a mobile phone outlet in a London suburb.

If I saw him in the street I wouldn't recognize him.

Any more than I'd recognize Kathleen.

Of course not.

Two days later I had already forgotten her. On the train to Paris I thought about the three days that had just gone by and I could not call up her face. Just her dyed blonde hair: you could see the dark roots. Just the opposite of Cécile Duffaut. Cécile Duffaut would never have dyed her hair.

I wonder if Kathleen still feels embarrassed. If in a relaxed moment, say, when she's at a barbecue with colleagues or in the car with her kids, she suddenly purses her lips and makes a face because her memory has swerved in that direction. Her husband, in the seat next to her, will look surprised. She'll wave her hand as if to say, it's nothing. Something she ate. She'll take a tablet when they get home. It will pass.

And what about me, did it pass?

Yes, it did. That's the worst thing about it.

I made up a whole bunch of stories.

That in France I was studying to become a helicopter pilot, to rescue stranded mountaineers. That sort of rubbish. And the more lies I told her, the more I started to believe it. At last I was becoming another person. Kathleen hadn't lost that sulky look she had when I went up to her, but nor had she walked away. She couldn't help but smile, sometimes, because of my accent. We were in the other room, in the chapel. It was much darker there, with red seats and dim lights. We could hear the music from the dance floor, muted, just the bass causing the walls to vibrate. Around us, only couples in various stages of intimacy. A back room in a church. The England I had hoped to see. Not the one where tourist couples wander through rooms in a museum or stroll through parks pointing at swans and daffodils.

She wanted to dance.

She was wearing one of those black lace dresses that

were in fashion. With a leopard skin scarf in her hair. Bold red lipstick. A come-hither sort of attitude. An ersatz Madonna let loose on the streets of London. One among thousands.

At one point she let out a graceless yawn, and I thought that was it, but she said it was just that she was tired, she'd had a rough week, she lived all the way on the edge of London, quite far away, there were no more trains or underground, the taxi would cost a fortune and in any case they would never agree to take her way out there at that hour of the night, was I staying at a hotel?

"Yes."

"Can we go there?"

"There's just one problem. I … actually, I'm sharing the room with my sister."

"Your sister?"

"Yes, we came to London together."

"Ah-hah."

"But she shouldn't be there anymore, she was supposed to leave for France this evening."

"So, what's the problem?"

"Right. Otherwise we can find a room in another hotel."

"I'm not a whore."

"I never said you were."

"Either we sleep at your place, or it's *nyet*."

"What, *nyet*?"

"Well, come on then."

I remember our walk through the London night.

We didn't talk. I didn't even know her last name. And everything she had learned about me was untrue. Anyway, she was no fool. She felt like spending the night with me and, while we were at it, she'd have a place to sleep. I prefer to think it went in that order.

While we were walking, I wondered if I could stop it right there. If I could explain and say, "Actually, Cécile and me, you see … I don't know what came over me. It's not right. Can we meet again tomorrow or another day? Really, tonight's no good, but I would really, truly, madly like to kiss your breasts."

But the words didn't come.

It took us half an hour to walk from the cathedral-temple of the night to Cartwright Gardens, and I found myself praying to the Holy Ghost that Cécile really had left in the end, and everything would be easy, we could make it up back in France, I would grovel before her with apologies, I would make promises, and she would never find out a thing about Kathleen No-Name. Or maybe the aforementioned Kathleen would remember a very important appointment at three o'clock in the morning, and she absolutely had to get back to her suburb, she would slip me her name and her phone number, and then she would say tomorrow, same time, and the next day at the same time I would be there, I would have dealt with the Cécile problem, Cécile would be gone, bag and baggage, bye now, air kisses on both cheeks, no hard feelings, right?

Sometimes, when you're twenty, you don't really know how to deal with certain situations.

Sometimes, when you're forty-seven, you're no better.

I am sitting next to Cécile, and I wish I could tell her I am sorry.

Even if it is no longer the least bit important now.

Even if what is important, now, is that I am on my way to see Mathieu, possibly for the last time.

And that all these years are rising up before me on this innocuous 6:41 train which has just gone past the huge shopping mall at Rosny 2. The Paris suburbs, spread out before me there just beyond the window: I could never live here.

And yet maybe my life would have been better, here.

I cannot stop the stream of images. And yet how I wish I could. I'm worn out. The weekend with my parents was worse than expected. It was the first time I've ever found them old, really old, not just older than me, but on the threshold of everything inevitable—physical decline, retirement home, dependency, everything I haven't wanted to think about until now, everything I have avoided by choosing for a companion an independent man who has no family ties. He cannot imagine living anywhere but Paris, he needs the big city, the capital, the constant movement of crowds, the noise, distraction, anonymity.

And the same has been true for me, up to now.

I moved to Paris later than he did. But I was in the same frame of mind. I wanted to be swept up by the crowd, I wanted to choose the people I met and no longer just put up with them because I had no choice—because in the provinces choices are limited and lives are stunted.

Now I'm not so sure of myself.

Valentine has become a Parisian adolescent, self-confident, aware of what is at stake, clued in about which friendships to avoid and which ones to nurture; she's learned the social codes, she's street-smart—and above all she's savvy, really savvy. Compared to her, at the same age, I was a goose. A goose who got roasted in the oven and carved to pieces. I'm proud of Valentine.

She won't ever be duped the way I was. I watch her. In her love affairs, her friendships, she's the one who's in charge. And I was the one, rather than Luc, who wanted her to be like that.

My mother trembles.

She didn't use to tremble. Her head trembles, when she's fixing a meal, and serving the food, and she doesn't realize, I would like to point it out, but I don't dare. I wonder if she's going to tremble more and more until her brain disintegrates. That's what I dreamed last night. I woke up with a start: I had just seen my mother in bits all over the carpet in the living room, like a broken and bleeding robot.

That night, too, I woke up with a start.

I heard voices, two of them. His voice I recognized immediately. But the other one: female. English. Annoyed. Saying something about his sister. Philippe Leduc's sister. I grasped the situation in instant. I sat up. I didn't need to reach for the covers. I had fallen asleep with all my clothes on. He'd switched on only the bedside lamp. The girl was in the dark. All I could see was her nightclub getup: an exact replica of Madonna in *Desperately Seeking Susan*. I thought about certain movies, saw myself as Rosanna Arquette in *After Hours*: the scene was insane, and the time of night was the same, according to the alarm clock: it was 3:30. I didn't need a diagram. I never thought he would stoop so low, but clearly with Philippe Leduc he could always go lower.

A few minutes.

It only lasted a few minutes.

I didn't say a single word.

Today this surprises me. I could have told him off, ranted, humiliated him, foamed at the mouth—but all I felt was disgust. Yes, that's what it was, disgust.

The disgust I felt when my grandfather, my father's father, would hit my grandmother. I used to spend the weekend with them from time to time. He wasn't even drunk. For him it was just normal behavior. When I told my mother about it, she refused to let me go back there. My father didn't insist. And yet the harm was done. My grandmother, cowering, trying to protect herself while I ran out to the barn for refuge.

The disgust I felt when I heard the father of my best friend and neighbor, Claudie, yelling insanely at his wife, a poor creature who was afraid of everything. He called her a whore, a sailor's slut, a chamber pot, there was no end to it. When I ran into Claudie, an hour later, we acted as if nothing had happened, but she knew that I knew, and she was filled with shame.

The disgust I felt toward that guy who was stalking me. I knew he had it in for me. At a party the previous month I had rejected his advances. I was at the lycée. The year before my final year. I was going down the avenue that led to the center of town. He was on a motorbike. He stopped the motor. The swishing of his tires on the asphalt. I was focusing on the sidewalk. I had been told you shouldn't look back, because it drives them crazy. I could feel my chin trembling, but I wouldn't cry, I would be strong. I had five hundred yards to go. His voice. My first name. The sound of the kickstand. He was running. He grabbed my arm. I wanted to shout, "What?" but the words stuck in my throat. He tried to kiss me. I hit him. He raised his hand. A man who was passing by shouted, "What's going on? Do you want me to call the police?" The guy's hand stayed where it was. He stepped back. He stumbled. The passerby waited by my side. The motorcycle started up. The man said, "You ought to report him." As he rode by, the boy on the motorcycle spat and called me a whore.

All that disgust.

All the instances of disgust you experience simply by virtue of being a girl.

And that night, you added one more, Philippe Leduc.

A pretty significant one, too.

Never had I felt like such a burden.

Or so humiliated.

I started getting ready, in heavy silence. Outside, even London was asleep. I straightened my clothes, splashed some water on my face, checked that I had my documents, my train ticket, the money I needed. Very professional. I felt like I was in a film, one of those black-and-white thrillers where the heroines sleep in motels and then disappear. I didn't feel a thing, other than an anticipation of fatigue, because it was 3:30 in the morning and I had to walk all the way to Waterloo Station, a long way, and the city at that time of night would be full of boys on motorcycles wanting to follow me. As I left the room I managed to call out, trying hard to make my voice sound bright, "Have a nice evening!" but I knew that for them, too, everything had been ruined. The girl was acting blasé, but beneath her makeup and her getup, she was worried. About me. She was wondering where I would go like that. She was drawing a kind of parallel between me and herself. A sisterhood. The word almost made me smile. As I walked by her, I whispered, "I'm not his sister, you know." But she already knew that—of course she knew. She had figured it all out.

Suddenly I was out in the street.

It was balmy, a horribly pleasant night.
London in July. If I'd been a smoker, I would have lit a cigarette.

I sat down on the bench across from the hotel and said, out loud, "Two minutes!"

Two minutes to catch my breath. Two minutes to change my life, too. And then, of course, I burst into tears. I was instantly annoyed with myself. I didn't want to be the caricature of the girl who's been dumped and goes to pieces. I didn't want to be like anyone, anymore. What I really wanted from then on was dignity and respect, and to be capable of insolence and determination.

I was sick and tired of being the ant.

I thought I'd try to find a place to spend the rest of the night—go to a park, walk through the damp grass, find refuge in a bush or under a tree, spread my towel for a mattress, use my backpack as a pillow, curl up and hope no one would approach me or attack me, and try to relax while I listened to the birds' waking song.

But once I started walking, I knew it wouldn't work out like that. As I walked through those London streets everything began to make sense. That girl's expression for a start, straight out of an American movie; then Philippe Leduc's, downcast, eyes averted. It was ridiculous. I sensed that I had to take it from there. That moment would be the sandbank—or shoal, rather—on which I had run aground, and now I would have to kick my heel against it to rise back up to the surface.

I built myself a future.

First of all, I would finish my studies: I'd been on the verge of letting them drag on and on, or of dropping them altogether, and they would have led nowhere. Now I would start learning, and then I'd learn some more. I would stop being the student who just scrapes by with average grades, and about whom people said, when they looked at the list of students who'd been promoted, "Huh, she actually passed?"

I would change where I lived, too—I'd move to a big city, where opportunities would be real and careers didn't lead down some dead-end street. To a place where I could still meet people by chance.

And above all, I would never allow myself to be impressed.

No matter the age, gender, history, or social position of the people I met, I would immediately treat them as equals. Human beings with the same genetic heritage—vulnerable to viruses, prone to sudden illness during a romantic weekend in Amsterdam, capable of humiliating a girl by bringing another one up to the room, and probably concealing a secret life, full of inadmissible vices, moments of distress, grimaces in the mirror, and disgust.

Then there were my looks, obviously.

Change things: a concession I had never wanted to make until now. Start using the makeup kits I sometimes bought but rarely opened, as if they weren't meant for me, as if I didn't deserve them.

Go to the hairdresser's. Get one of those boyish cuts that were suddenly cropping up in the photos in hairdressing salons.

Do something about my wardrobe.

Oh yes, my wardrobe.

Throw out anything shapeless, all-purpose, beige, brown, sea-green, gray, or blue. Start trying bright colors, accentuate the red, yellow, and orange, learn to stand out.

If I close my eyes, I can still see those London streets, that sweltering July night.

Of course I passed a few night owls, but they didn't notice me. Just wait a few years, I thought, and then they'll turn around when I go by. At one point I got lost on my way to Waterloo. I went in circles for a few minutes. Twice walked past the only store whose display windows weren't protected by iron shutters. A boutique that sold herbs, and face creams made from plants, and makeup that was one hundred percent natural. It seemed ever so amateurish, like some holdover from the seventies, people living in communes—completely out of sync with the triumphalist eighties, a rotten tooth that needed pulling. It suddenly occurred to me: if I were in charge of that store, I would organize everything differently, make it modern, make it popular. No, not popular, better than that. Trendy. Upmarket.

For thirty seconds or so I saw through to my future—and then the door slammed shut. It took me more than fifteen years to open it again. They weren't lost years. It took me that long to come to terms with everything I was feeling that night.

A desire for revenge; pride, determination, and even a sort of feverish joy. A joy that vanished the minute the sun came up. A joy which, on the train home, gave way to that electrifying hatred. Which spread all through my body. A hatred which left a lasting trace. A hatred which, much later, only Luc managed to extinguish—even though, in the beginning, all I wanted was to seduce him, the better to drop him not long afterward. To leave him reeling. Gasping. Needy. Like all the others, after Leduc and before Luc, whom I had unceremoniously dumped.

I never went back to London. I've visited half the planet, and I've always taken great care to avoid the United Kingdom.

Would I be ready to go back there now?
Would I be ready to forgive?

It still gets to me.

I may claim that it doesn't. That it's just some unpleasant memory I can brush aside. That would be true, too. I don't dwell on it. But there are times when that night comes back to me. I'll be shaving, looking in the mirror, telling myself I've gone downhill, that I look like an obese, wrinkled caricature of Hugh Grant in *Four Weddings and a Funeral*—and my mind wanders as I pull at my skin, and the razor tries to restore a semblance of youth to my cheeks and my neck. Then all of a sudden, my lips pucker with a bitter taste. I can see myself outside the stadium in Aube, I'm twelve years old, and I've just made Karima cry, telling her that I don't talk to foreigners. Or I'm sixteen and I've just told off a classmate because he's worried about his mother, the chemo is really rough going, and I shouted at him that he was a pain, couldn't he stop making such a big deal out of it? I don't know what came over me. Then I'm twenty, there are two girls in a hotel room, it's dead quiet, and one of them walks past the other and says, "I'm not his sister, you know."

What do other people do to forget?

One day I started looking to see if there wasn't some sort of group therapy, an Alcoholics Anonymous type meeting, where everyone would sit and hold hands and say their name—hello, I'm Philippe—and where you could off-load your most shameful memories. I couldn't find anything. Maybe I didn't look hard enough. That's my problem, after all. I don't look hard enough. I wait for the fruit to fall fully ripened from the tree. Stewed. For a while, it worked. But now I lack confidence in myself. No, that's not exactly it, either. I don't trust myself. That's why I'm going to see Mathieu at the hospital.

Because Mathieu is at death's door, and he trusts me. And it feels good.

It's repugnant.

I could tell her, Cécile, about Mathieu. But she probably doesn't remember him. They crossed paths only because of me. When I was going out with her, I saw a lot less of him. She must have met him two or three times at most, at parties, where they hardly spoke. He thought she wasn't much to look at. He couldn't understand why I was wasting my time with her. When I came back from London, I simply told him that it was over, he nodded, and we never spoke of it again.

I can't believe it.

We can't go our separate ways like this, with me getting to my feet, and her sitting there, and me saying, "Have a nice time in Paris!" and getting off the train. It's idiotic, I have to do something, it's my only chance. If only I had a business card. I've always been impressed by business cards. These people you hardly know, and after only a few minutes talking to them they hand you a card with their name and address, you don't really know why, what do they expect, for you to call them? For you to go and have a drink together, and become friends or even more if you get along? And yet the fact remains I wish I had one now.

These days our kids have it easier. Manon and Loïc just tell someone that they're on Facebook or Twitter, and the other person nods, and that very evening they're virtual friends, and they know all about each other's lives, their likes and interests, their professional situation. I'm not on Facebook. At one point I wanted to sign up—my kids couldn't believe their ears. I toyed with the idea for a while and then on reflection I wondered who I would contact on a social network. Mathieu's friends? Forgotten classmates? Colleagues I see every day anyway? It seemed pointless. I abandoned the idea. But now Paris is getting closer, and on our right you can just see the outline of Sacré-Coeur between two tall buildings, and I'm beginning to feel real panic.

I can't go on letting things slip away from me. I can see the years ahead—like railroad tracks stretching into the distance, as far as the station. I meet people, and then they're gone. And all that's left is the debris they leave behind—remnants of shared lunches, hastily drunk coffees, snatches of conversation, murmurs.

It hurts.
There, in my chest.
Between my ribs.
I'm not scared. I'm used to it. It's been waking me up at night for the last few months. I mentioned it to the

doctor, he shrugged, he asked me if there was anything bothering me. It's nerves, he added. Nothing out of the ordinary.

I'm nervous.

And nothing out of the ordinary.

That night was probably even more unexceptional than the others. Pathetic. Kathleen didn't ask a single question after Cécile left. She just wanted to lie down and go to sleep. You could hear the birds in the little park across from the hotel. She got undressed very quickly and lay down on her back. She didn't seem to care one way or the other about what was about to happen. It was depressing. As for me, I tried to revive a bit, but it didn't go very far. By tacit agreement we didn't take the experiment any further. She fell asleep almost at once. I didn't. I lay staring at the ceiling—it had recently been repainted, it looked like a rush job. The day that had just gone by flickered past my eyes, but I couldn't make any sense of it. I just wondered how I had come to this.

Apparently there are people who, at a certain time in their life, get the impression they're touching bottom and then mentally, they kick the floor with their heel to go back up. I've never believed in that sort of nonsense. Because it's never happened to me. I didn't get the feeling I was headed back toward the light, either the next morning, or in the days that followed. I woke up at noon, and Kathleen had left, the room was paid for two more nights, so I hung around London. I wrote two or three letters, to Cécile, to Mathieu, but I didn't send them, I forgot them at the hotel. I must have done that deliberately.

I went back to France.

Life went on.

The defiance only came gradually. I knew I was capable of shabby betrayals, of low-down tricks. Whenever I started going out with a girl who was willing and eager, I tried to make her understand that I wasn't worth it. And when we broke up, I would point out that I had warned her. But that never prevented the crying, the tears, the insults—on the contrary, the more they knew I was right, the more they hauled me over the coals.

And then at one point I just gave up.

I was twenty-seven, I was a TV and VCR salesman at a superstore, I was living in a cheap and reasonably comfortable two-room apartment; one evening, I sat by the window in the kitchen and I said to myself, Okay, I think I've had enough. I didn't feel like meeting anyone—all the hoops you had to jump through, pretending to admire or understand—I would rather just fade into the background and let the world go about its business—it would be easier that way. I was tired. That's it. Yes. Exhausted, even. I met my wife six months later. That's what she liked about me, right from the start, my fatigue. My disillusionment. And consequently, my candor. She took up the challenge. My wife is something of a Pygmalion. She wanted to restore my fighting spirit.

And eventually she gave up.

I understand her oh so well.

But along the way, we did have two children together. That counts for something. That's what I keep telling myself, every day. It's not nothing. I still count for something.

Ouch.

It's almost as if someone were snipping at my lungs with very fine scissors.

I have to stretch—as a rule, that eases the pain.

Like that, yesss.

Uh-oh. I bumped into Cécile Duffaut.

"Excuse me, I'm sorry."
"No problem."

Silence.
Loudspeaker crackling.
Our train will be arriving shortly in Paris, Gare de l'Est, our final station. On behalf of the SNCF, the train manager, and crew hope you have had a pleasant journey.

"I am really sorry."
"It's not a problem, really, it was nothing."
"No, that's not what I mean. What I mean is, I'm sorry about everything. About what happened almost thirty years ago. About London. I am. I'm really sorry."
"Oh. Thank you."

At least now it's done.

I expect it's something Mathieu would have done, too. That's how he must be feeling these days, wishing he could ease his conscience. Put an end to all the failures, tie up all the loose ends. When you're at death's door, you won't be in the mood for Impressionists. Vermeer would be more like it. *A View of Delft*, say. Or any seventeenth century Dutch interior. Or why not Bacon's screaming popes or decomposing bodies, while you're at it.

I don't know how he's doing.

Yesterday on the phone he was totally delirious. Half in tears over a red bicycle he used to have when he was nine years old, and half elated because he's convinced that he'll be going home soon. I'm glad his mother is not altogether lucid anymore. I couldn't stand seeing any of my children die before me.

I got hold of the head nurse on the phone. She knows me. She knows I'm a substitute family. I'm everything at once: parents, brother, son, friend. Even though Mathieu and I stopped seeing each other for almost twenty years. It's pathetic. She told me they'd increased the dose of morphine, and that his delirium might be a consequence of the injections, unless the metastasis has already reached his brain. They would have to check, with a scan. There was a moment of silence. She murmured, "If it comes to that." I understood that I had to get there as fast as I could.

So here I am.

Whatever Cécile Duffaut might think, I'm very loyal. It's probably my best quality: for anyone I get attached to, or who gets attached to me, I'm like a dog. It's not a very sexy trait, I'll grant you that. It's not the sort of thing you can let slip in conversation, when you meet someone. "You know, I'm very loyal": you might as well tell them that you collect ceramic owls or that you spend your Sunday afternoons in front of the TV.

Cécile Duffaut doesn't give a damn. She doesn't give a damn about what I just told her.

At the same time, I can hardly say I blame her. It was twenty-seven years ago. A whole lifetime has gone by since then. There's no point talking about it anymore. Or apologizing.

Thank God the trip will be over soon.

Sorry.

It was kind of him to say it.

To say he was sorry.

And I said, thank you.

How stupid.

Either you say nothing, and you cloak yourself in your dignity, you cast a scornful look at the odious individual who has dared to speak to you; or you accept the apology and you continue the conversation, Oh, and how are you after all these years, are you married, do you have kids, where do you work, well, you see, you made your way after all.

But like an imbecile, I dithered, somewhere in between.

I suppose that's just the way I react to him—I'm indecisive, half stunned, half annoyed, incapable of deciding anything until the facts shove me out the door. Off the train. Out of the hotel room.

Why am I hung up on the past when I should be forging ahead, elated, looking forward to whatever's in store? That's how things were until last year. But now some spring has lost its tension; there's some mechanism that hasn't seized up yet, but it's creaking. It's harder to stifle those yawns in the morning. Valentine is almost seventeen, and she's slipping away—and with her, the strongest tie I have with Luc. I wonder what will be left of our relationship once our daughter has left home. Maybe we'll just congratulate each other, with kisses on both cheeks: "You did good with the kid, we can be proud, I'm off now, ciao," and go our separate ways without any other due process, because for a long time now we haven't exactly known who we are to each other, what we like, what we want. Or we'll go on living together, like mussels on a rock, waiting for the next tide.

Balance sheet.
Settling of accounts.
That's what I've been going over these last few months.
My life, two columns: pluses and minuses.
This I like / this I don't like.
Make lists of what you like / what bothers you.
I sound like an article in a woman's magazine.
I hate that sort of thing.

My father was a genealogy fanatic.
It started when he was about forty-five; I was still at the lycée. He would spend his vacations writing letters, making phone calls, going from one town hall to the next to look at birth registries. I was laughing behind his back. I couldn't have been happier. While he was busy doing that he was off my case, and I was free to come and go as I pleased. Otherwise he'd spend all day telling me to "go out for some air," or "do something intelligent." I still don't understand what he meant by that, coming from him, a man who didn't read or listen

to music and who'd never set foot in a museum. For him intelligent was probably a synonym for useful: housework, mending, shopping.

This lasted until his retirement; I thought he'd have something to keep him busy once he stopped work, that he'd continue to pursue his passion, go all the way back to the sixteenth century, fill in his family trees. But all of a sudden he lost interest. The family trees must be in some dusty corner of the attic.

I've never been like him. I've never wanted to pore over registries of births, deaths, and marriages just to find out that one of my ancestors was a blacksmith. I'm much more down to earth than that. Now things have changed somewhat. We have, imperceptibly, grown closer. Just as everything has begun to take off professionally for me— we're opening new stores, the business is booming—I've begun to feel a sort of weariness. All I want to do, in fact, is sit in a deck chair on an evening in June and start to drop off right there, just as the night is falling, and I'll be vaguely trying to remember the names of the stars above me. The way he used to. One day, perhaps, we'll be able to name them together. At last.

I wonder if Philippe has any aspirations. Probably not. Philippe isn't the aspiring kind. He seizes the moment and consequences be damned. He must cheat on his wife, and his kids will think he's a hero, what with the pointless but entertaining conversations I'm sure they have together.

What if I dare to look him right in the face.

My eyes trained right on him.

Deep, unattractive wrinkles. His hair beginning to thin. And that paunch, above all. I assumed, naïvely, that he would stay slim as he got old. That he'd be one of those crisp fiftysomething men who go running every Sunday and don't put on an ounce of fat even when they give up smoking. Like Luc. Or like that friend of his, Mathieu Coché. Now there's a good-looking man. Good-looking, and not such an unpleasant memory in the end. Maybe I could start with that. A benign conversation, now that the train has stopped for a few minutes before it pulls into the station: we can see Sacré-Coeur on the right, and the Cité des Sciences on the left. An empty conversation of the kind he must enjoy, and which would at least have the advantage of not letting our non-encounter end on the unpleasant note of an unconfirmed request for forgiveness. Something like, "I saw your friend Mathieu Coché in a magazine the other day." His eyes would light up. Even if they haven't seen each other in ages. It's always nice to have a friend who's famous. It makes your own star shine a little brighter.

Yes, I could try that. Two minutes exchanging bland information, and we would say good-bye with a smile.

I'll be magnanimous.

I need my peace of mind.

We regret to inform our passengers that the train is currently stopped on the tracks and we ask that you do not try to open the doors. The train will be moving again shortly.

Grumbling and muttering up and down the train.
Sighs.
"Shit, we were almost there. That's the SNCF for you."

Or the SNCF, maybe.

A stock phrase like the one the guy in front of me just said: "That's the SNCF for you." Everyone is nodding and grumbling. Everyone complains about the SNCF, in a spirit of consensus, criticizing everyone and no one at the same time, and it gives us plenty of excuses for being in a bad mood, it's manna from heaven for those who firmly believe the country is going to the dogs, that everything was better before, and now we're in the gutter about to be washed down the drain, splash.

I had a bad taste in my mouth.

But the SNCF would still be a good way to try and break the ice. Let her fly off the handle and rant and rave if she needs to. At least so we don't part on an unpleasant note.

Make small talk.

I would love to make small talk with Cécile Duffaut. At a sidewalk café overlooking the Canal Saint-Martin, or on the Boulevard Saint-Germain.

Before or after the hospital.

After would be better. To get my life back to normal. Yes, that's it. To get my life back to normal.

"I saw your—"

"The SNCF is—"

"I'm sorry, what were you saying?"

"Excuse me, I interrupted—"

A blank.

A jolt.

Two jolts.

A sigh.

The train has started moving again.

In front of us, behind us, the passengers on the 6:41 train, due to arrive at the Gare de l'Est at 8:15, are getting to their feet, taking their luggage down from the overhead rack, rubbing their eyes, wiping their hands over their faces, blinking, and getting their bearings: station platform, Métro, stairs, sidewalks, two hundred yards, building, office, quick coffee from the machine, good morning to all and sundry, files, debriefing, slightly tense smile, another week has begun.

They're intimidating, all these passengers standing one behind the other waiting for the line to start moving, to alight from the train, watch the steps, place their feet on the asphalt and begin the race. They clear their throats, check their watches for the twentieth time. They have little tics: they scratch the top of their eyebrows, or their neck, or their earlobe. They are drawing up their lists of things to do. People to see. The chorus of names. And in the middle of all that, incongruously, their spouses, their children—the people they'll see only too briefly, until next weekend.

They're so intimidating that you don't dare look at them. And since Cécile Duffaut and Philippe Leduc don't dare look at each other, either, they are staring at the dirty floor of the train: there's a grayish pink wad of crushed chewing gum, an empty bottle of mineral water. They're sorry they ever started that conversation: What were they thinking?

Or maybe they're sorry they didn't start it earlier. They're a bit puzzled. A bit lost. They can't quite tell what will happen next. They are about to look up and speak again at the same time, but Cécile Duffaut senses this, and she gets there first. She says, "I saw your friend, Mathieu Coché—well, I don't know if he's still your friend, but the friend that you used to have, anyway, way back when. In a magazine. I saw him in a magazine."

She feels like a complete idiot.

She has repeated the word "friend" three times. And "magazine" twice.

She can see the red ink, her ninth-grade French teacher crossing out all her repetitions and writing in the margin, "Expand your vocabulary, for goodness' sake!!!" With all those exclamation marks. That was the most humiliating thing about it, all those exclamation marks. You always feel crushed by an exclamation mark. It's like a stone falling from a wall—and you're standing right in its path. Why did she suddenly think of that, just now?

Why did she bring up Mathieu Coché?

Check out the expression on Philippe Leduc's face.

As if an entire army of exclamation marks had tumbled down upon him.

"He … I'm on my way to see him."

"Sorry?"

"That's why I'm on this train, I'm going to see him."

"Oh. That's great. Tell him I said hello. Although I'm not sure he'll remember me."

"He's in the hospital."

"Oh dear. I hope it's not serious?"

"He's dying. That's why I'm going to see him. Because he's going to die. Any day. So, I'm going to see him. You know what I mean?"

She doesn't answer. She doesn't know what to say. As if she's driven down a one-way street the wrong way. There's a part of her that would like to continue the conversation, "Oh, look at that graffiti under the bridge, that's original, isn't it? Have you seen any good films recently?" But suddenly there is police tape everywhere, like in a crime film, a flimsy barrier that stops you going any farther and above all entering the scene of the crime. She can no longer put any words to what she feels. She is standing across from this imbecile whose eyes have misted over, and she's not doing so great herself, the corners of her eyes are stinging, it's idiotic, over someone she hardly knew almost thirty years ago, no, it makes no sense. She frowns: that ought to send any threatening tears in another direction. She murmurs, "What does he have?" and in her mind, a succession of images: hospital corridors, blood tests, surgeons' faces, HIV, scanners, bodies entering a tunnel, George Clooney in *E.R.* Philippe Leduc tilts his head and says, "Cancer. Terminal, obviously." And there are all those people going by with their bags, their suitcases, their briefcases, where are they going, which Métro station, what will happen to them today, who knows, maybe one of them has just taken their last train ride, and they don't know it yet, but it was their last ride, and later on, they'll be crossing a busy street without paying attention, and boom, it's all over, move along now, there's nothing to see.

Philippe is brave. He pulls himself together. She has no way of knowing all he's been through over the last ninety-five minutes, on the train. She has no way of knowing that he has revisited it all, that he has been back to London. That is also why his eyes filled with tears all of a sudden. He apologizes. He's annoyed with himself, too. He would like, one day, to be able to stop apologizing. Now, awkwardly, he tries to get the conversation going again.

"And you … what brings you to Paris?"

But all these people are getting off and soon the car will be empty, it's so late, it's much too late. She replies, "I work here. I live here," getting to her feet at the same time, and Philippe moves to one side. But he doesn't give in. Now that he's taken the first step, he presses on. He asks her if she has children. It is so totally irrelevant, completely out of left field, that Cécile

Duffaut cannot help but smile and say, "Yes. A daughter. She's all grown-up now. At the lycée." She wants to get her bag from the luggage rack but he's quicker than she is. He takes the opportunity to tell her that he also has children, two of them, grown-up now, too, it's strange, isn't it?

"What's strange?"

"When we were younger, we never imagined that we'd have kids one day."

This time she laughs. She can't help it. He opens his eyes wide. He doesn't see what's so funny. She waves her hand as if to say, "Never mind, it's nothing," and then she does something, she places her hand on his shoulder, the way a father would, or a friend, or a brother, and it's very unsettling. In a kindly tone, she adds, "It's much too late to get to know each other again, and I don't take this train very often. I don't know if we'll meet again. Take care."

"Take care."

He's always hated that expression. It is one of his mother's favorite stock phrases, she uses it with everyone—neighbors, mailman, baker, son, nephews, brother, butcher at the supermarket, husband back in the day. Everyone is entitled to take care: of their activities, their everyday business, minor dramas, minor joys, the world is a crowd of plastic Playmobil figures jerkily waving their arms, spouting off from their invisible mouths, hearing without ears, their hair always impeccably styled, and they go about their assigned business, all of them, ceaselessly, taking care, it's good, to take care, it's fine.

And it's the same for all those people who, one after the other, have left the railroad car, they are taking care, that's good, they're making calls on their cell phones to say when they'll be there, they're sending text messages so others know they've gotten off the train, they fiddle with their earphones, their touch screens, the keys on the keyboard, they're clicking and communicating yet there's not a sound, just a hollowness, they are merely indicating that they are taking care and that's good, I'm taking care and that's good, everything is collapsing all around me, worse than that, everything is made of cardboard, of putty, of plastic, the hospital is a bed with a thermometer but I'm a nurse, I wear a blue helmet with a transparent visor and carry a truncheon so I'm a policeman, I have a hammer and a hard hat so I'm a builder—I don't have any questions to ask, I know what I have to do, I'm taking care and that's good, I always take care and that's good, and get on with it, get on with it, you have to get on with it.

"Coffee?"

"No … I think … I don't think that's a good idea."

"What makes you so sure?"

"I'm not. I'm not so sure. It's just that this sort of thing happens all the time, people who knew each other briefly a long time ago and they run into each other, and there's nothing more to say, you think about it for a few minutes and then you go back to your routine, there's no reason why you should change it."

"You basically go on taking care of things."

"Yes, that's it."

"I hope you'll have a thought for me before you die."

Cécile Duffaut is shocked. Almost as much by the words as by the general appearance of the man standing across from her. He seems to be projecting a sort of violence she would never have imagined. Violence but also, oh God, she doesn't want to admit it, but yes, all the same, never mind if it seems hackneyed, yes, he's projecting sensuality, the sensuality of 8:15 in the morning, on the platform at the Gare de l'Est, it's hardly the place for it, after all. There he is, he's desperate, like a dog about to bite, she has to leave now, she's right, she knows she is, she has to go. Her brain is teeming with words, snatches of phrases, fragments of images, if she were Valentine, she'd give him her email, digital makes things easier, it leaves a trace and yet at the same time leaves no trace, it's magical, but now is not the time for magical thinking, get going now, move.

She picks up her bag. She shifts her shoulder so it will hang properly, she smoothes her skirt which had ridden up slightly, she's not looking at him anymore, she turns around and heads for the exit, she's searching for something to say, she ought to be able to come up with some ironic quip about fate, misfortune, destiny, something that would hit home, but she can't find anything, it's hopeless, she keeps walking, there's nothing left, it's incredible how there's nothing left, it's a desert, a green desert, the Périgord, the Lot, rocks, oak trees, walnut trees, a river, a river through the Gare de l'Est, what on earth, railway tracks, there's nothing but railway tracks and the imperturbable voice announcing platforms, arrivals, departures, delays, because oh yes, there are plenty of delays, and sometimes the trains stop altogether, somewhere they are not taking care to keep things going, and that's not good, not to take care, not good at all.

Then, ever so slowly, she stops. She is next to car number three. She doesn't turn around. Seen from behind—her shoulders drooping only slightly, her handbag swinging dangerously, her fingers relaxing, she has paused to take a deep breath. Her legs don't move. She is still facing toward the central hall of the station, and there are hundreds of thighs, elbows, bellies, feet, and hips hurrying past her. She has stopped. She's not taking care. She is going to turn around. No one knows if it will be a good thing.

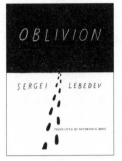

OBLIVION BY SERGEI LEBEDEV

In one of the first 21st century Russian novels to probe the legacy of the Soviet prison camp system, a young man travels to the vast wastelands of the Far North to uncover the truth about a shadowy neighbor who saved his life, and whom he knows only as Grandfather II. Emerging from today's Russia, where the ills of the past are being forcefully erased from public memory, this masterful novel represents an epic literary attempt to rescue history from the brink of oblivion.

ON THE RUN WITH MARY BY JONATHAN BARROW

Shining moments of tender beauty punctuate this story of a youth on the run after escaping from an elite English boarding school. At London's Euston Station, the narrator meets a talking dachshund named Mary and together they're off on escapades through posh Mayfair streets and jaunts in a Rolls-Royce. But the youth soon realizes that the seemingly sweet dog is a handful; an alcoholic, nymphomaniac, drug-addicted mess who can't stay out of pubs or off the dance floor. *On the Run with Mary* mirrors the horrors and the joys of the terrible 20th century.

THE LAST WEYNFELDT BY MARTIN SUTER

Adrian Weynfeldt is an art expert in an international auction house, a bachelor in his mid-fifties living in a grand Zurich apartment filled with costly paintings and antiques. Always correct and well-mannered, he's given up on love until one night—entirely out of character for him—Weynfeldt decides to take home a ravishing but unaccountable young woman and gets embroiled in an art forgery scheme that threatens his buttoned up existence. This refined page-turner moves behind elegant bourgeois facades into darker recesses of the heart.

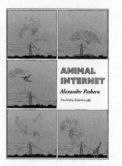

ANIMAL INTERNET BY ALEXANDER PSCHERA

Some 50,000 creatures around the globe—including whales, leopards, flamingoes, bats and snails—are being equipped with digital tracking devices. The data gathered and studied by major scientific institutes about their behavior will warn us about tsunamis, earthquakes and volcanic eruptions, but also radically transform our relationship to the natural world. Contrary to pessimistic fears, author Alexander Pschera sees the Internet as creating a historic opportunity for a new dialogue between man and nature.

GUYS LIKE ME BY DOMINIQUE FABRE

Dominique Fabre, born in Paris and a life-long resident of the city, exposes the shadowy, anonymous lives of many who inhabit the French capital. In this quiet, subdued tale, a middle-aged office worker, divorced and alienated from his only son, meets up with two childhood friends who are similarly adrift. He's looking for a second act to his mournful life, seeking the harbor of love and a true connection with his son. Set in palpably real Paris streets that feel miles away from the City of Light, a stirring novel of regret and absence, yet not without a glimmer of hope.

KILLING AUNTIE BY ANDRZEJ BURSA

A young university student named Jurek, with no particular ambitions or talents, finds himself with nothing to do. After his doting aunt asks the young man to perform a small chore, he decides to kill her for no good reason other than, perhaps, boredom. This short comedic masterpiece combines elements of Dostoevsky, Sartre, Kafka, and Heller, coming together to produce an unforgettable tale of murder and—just maybe—redemption.

I Called Him Necktie by Milena Michiko Flašar

Twenty-year-old Taguchi Hiro has spent the last two years of his life living as a hikikomori—a shut-in who never leaves his room and has no human interaction—in his parents' home in Tokyo. As Hiro tentatively decides to reenter the world, he spends his days observing life from a park bench. Gradually he makes friends with Ohara Tetsu, a salaryman who has lost his job. The two discover in their sadness a common bond. This beautiful novel is moving, unforgettable, and full of surprises.

Who is Martha? by Marjana Gaponenko

In this rollicking novel, 96-year-old ornithologist Luka Levadski foregoes treatment for lung cancer and moves from Ukraine to Vienna to make a grand exit in a luxury suite at the Hotel Imperial. He reflects on his past while indulging in Viennese cakes and savoring music in a gilded concert hall. Levadski was born in 1914, the same year that Martha—the last of the now-extinct passenger pigeons—died. Levadski himself has an acute sense of being the last of a species. This gloriously written tale mixes piquant wit with lofty musings about life, friendship, aging and death.

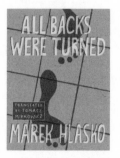

All Backs Were Turned by Marek Hlasko

Two desperate friends—on the edge of the law—travel to the southern Israeli city of Eilat to find work. There, Dov Ben Dov, the handsome native Israeli with a reputation for causing trouble, and Israel, his sidekick, stay with Ben Dov's younger brother, Little Dov, who has enough trouble of his own. Local toughs are encroaching on Little Dov's business, and he enlists his older brother to drive them away. It doesn't help that a beautiful German widow is rooming next door. A story of passion, deception, violence, and betrayal, conveyed in hard-boiled prose reminiscent of Hammett and Chandler.

ALEXANDRIAN SUMMER BY YITZHAK GORMEZANO GOREN

This is the story of two Jewish families living their frenzied last days in the doomed cosmopolitan social whirl of Alexandria just before fleeing Egypt for Israel in 1951. The conventions of the Egyptian upper-middle class are laid bare in this dazzling novel, which exposes sexual hypocrisies and portrays a vanished polyglot world of horse racing, seaside promenades and nightclubs.

COCAINE BY PITIGRILLI

Paris in the 1920s—dizzy and decadent. Where a young man can make a fortune with his wits ... unless he is led into temptation. Cocaine's dandified hero Tito Arnaudi invents lurid scandals and gruesome deaths, and sells these stories to the newspapers. But his own life becomes even more outrageous when he acquires three demanding mistresses. Elegant, witty and wicked, Pitigrilli's classic novel was first published in Italian in 1921 and retains its venom even today.

KILLING THE SECOND DOG BY MAREK HLASKO

Two down-and-out Polish con men living in Israel in the 1950s scam an American widow visiting the country. Robert, who masterminds the scheme, and Jacob, who acts it out, are tough, desperate men, exiled from their native land and adrift in the hot, nasty underworld of Tel Aviv. Robert arranges for Jacob to run into the widow who has enough trouble with her young son to keep her occupied all day. What follows is a story of romance, deception, cruelty and shame. Hlasko's writing combines brutal realism with smoky, hard-boiled dialogue, in a bleak world where violence is the norm and love is often only an act.

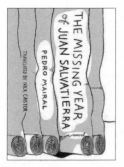

THE MISSING YEAR OF JUAN SALVATIERRA BY PEDRO MAIRAL

At the age of nine, Juan Salvatierra became mute following a horse riding accident. At twenty, he began secretly painting a series of canvases on which he detailed six decades of life in his village on Argentina's frontier with Uruguay. After his death, his sons return to deal with their inheritance: a shed packed with rolls over two miles long. But an essential roll is missing. A search ensues that illuminates links between art and life, with past family secrets casting their shadows on the present.

THE GOOD LIFE ELSEWHERE BY VLADIMIR LORCHENKOV

The very funny—and very sad—story of a group of villagers and their tragicomic efforts to emigrate from Europe's most impoverished nation to Italy for work. An Orthodox priest is deserted by his wife for an art-dealing atheist; a mechanic redesigns his tractor for travel by air and sea; and thousands of villagers take to the road on a modern-day religious crusade to make it to the Italian Promised Land. A country where 25 percent of its population works abroad, remittances make up nearly 40 percent of GDP, and alcohol consumption per capita is the world's highest – Moldova surely has its problems. But, as Lorchenkov vividly shows, it's also a country whose residents don't give up easily.

SOME DAY BY SHEMI ZARHIN

On the shores of Israel's Sea of Galilee lies the city of Tiberias, a place bursting with sexuality and longing for love. The air is saturated with smells of cooking and passion. *Some Day* is a gripping family saga, a sensual and emotional feast that plays out over decades. This is an enchanting tale about tragic fates that disrupt families and break our hearts. Zarhin's hypnotic writing renders a painfully delicious vision of individual lives behind Israel's larger national story.

Fanny von Arnstein: Daughter of the
***Enlightenment* by Hilde Spiel**

In 1776 Fanny von Arnstein, the daughter of
the Jewish master of the royal mint in Berlin,
came to Vienna as an 18-year-old bride. She
married a financier to the Austro-Hungarian
imperial court, and hosted an ever more
splendid salon which attracted luminaries of
the day. Spiel's elegantly written and carefully
researched biography provides a vivid portrait
of a passionate woman who advocated for the rights of Jews, and
illuminates a central era in European cultural and social history.

New Vessel Press

To purchase these titles and for more information please visit newvesselpress.com.